Bad Bella

Also by Ali Standish

The Ethan I Was Before
August Isle

Bad Bella

by Ali Standish

HARPER

An Imprint of HarperCollinsPublishers

www.harpercollinschildrens.com

ISBN 978-0-06-289325-3

Typography by Laura Mock
19 20 21 22 23 PC/LSCH 10 9 8 7 6 5 4 3 2 1

❖

First Edition

For all the good eggs
who have ever been called bad ones.

And of course for Bella,
the very best dog I could ever ask for.

Contents

One

The McBrides

Bella was the best of all the McBride children.

She never said it, of course. She wouldn't want to hurt the other children's feelings.

But she knew it was true.

It wasn't very hard, to be honest. She didn't have much competition.

The baby threw tantrums every night, her sister refused to do her chores, and her brother, who was the oldest, always left his muddy sneakers on the living-room floor and pulled away when Mrs. McBride tried to kiss him on the forehead.

Bella did none of these things. She never woke the McBrides up in the night, even when she couldn't sleep. She cleaned the crumbs from the kitchen floor every day without even being asked. She didn't wear sneakers and would love to be kissed on the forehead, only it seemed like nobody had tried for a long time now.

What's more, Bella never whined about what was for breakfast or dinner. She didn't get angry when her brother whacked her over her head with his stuffed dinosaur, or when her sister tied her ears together with an itchy pink bow.

What more could anyone ask of a child?

The McBrides had seemed pleased with Bella when they first brought her home (from where, Bella didn't know—she assumed all children wondered this). They were always cuddling her or playing with her, and even sharing their popcorn with her on movie night.

Popcorn, with extra butter, was Bella's favorite food.

But as the months went on and Bella grew bigger, they had started paying less and less attention to her and more and more attention to other things, like the television and their computers and their vacation plans for next summer.

Well then, thought Bella, *I must simply try harder to be a good girl.*

So she offered to play catch with Mrs. McBride to relax her before work, and always tried to lick her brother's feet clean when they got dirty. When there was a thunderstorm outside, she curled up on Mr. McBride's lap to keep him from being afraid. When her sister lost her teddy bear, Bella left *her* favorite toy—a rubber pig, only slightly covered in slobber—in her sister's backpack to lift her spirits. And one night, when the baby was crying and no one woke up, Bella slipped into his room and left half a biscuit she had been saving in his crib, just in case he was hungry.

But no matter how hard Bella tried to show the McBrides what a good girl she was, it never seemed to be enough. Mrs. McBride cringed at the sight of Bella's tennis ball. Her brother jerked his feet away from Bella's tongue. Mr. McBride scolded her to get off the couch. Her sister screamed when she found Bella's pig. The baby probably would have thanked Bella if he had known how, but he didn't. And anyway, Mrs. McBride had come in soon after Bella and thrown the biscuit in the trash before the baby had the chance to eat it.

"Bad Bella!" each of them had cried. (Except the baby, of course.)

Yes, Bella was the best of all the McBride children.

Only no one seemed to know this but her.

But I can't get discouraged, Bella often told herself. If there was one thing she was certain of, it was that the McBrides loved her. Someday they would finally notice how good she was, and things would start to change.

Then, one day, the tree came.

And things *did* change.

They got much, much worse.

꙳

It's not that Bella had anything against trees. Trees were fine, on the whole. They ranked in her top three places to go to the bathroom, along with the playground sandbox and the next-door neighbor's prizewinning rosebushes.

But everything might have been all right if it hadn't been for the tree. The spindly, prickly, seasick-green tree that stood almost to the ceiling, casting a dark shadow over Mrs. McBride's best rug.

It was after the McBrides brought the tree into the living room that things went from bad to worse. So Bella felt there was a good chance that everything that came after only happened because of the tree.

The day after its arrival, Mrs. McBride began talking on the phone all the time. She would huff and say things like "They'll have to make do with the pull-out couch," or "We've always had turkey, and we aren't going to switch to ham this year!"

The thought of turkey *or* ham was lovely enough to make Bella sigh with contentment, but the frown on Mrs. McBride's face only darkened.

While she spoke, she would move items of furniture around and sweep the floor underneath. And then she might interrupt herself and say, "Would you look at all the hair Bella has shed? I could stuff a whole pillow with it. And that's not even counting what I vacuum off my best rug every week."

Which made Bella feel very proud indeed.

The other strange thing about Mrs. McBride was that she seemed to be swelling up like a balloon. Every day her stomach got rounder, and she would often pat it and call it "little one." This made no sense because there was nothing little about Mrs. McBride's stomach.

Bella never said this, of course. She wouldn't want to hurt Mrs. McBride's feelings.

Meanwhile, Mr. McBride would disappear for hours at a time and come home with piles of shopping bags, which he shoved under the bed or on the top shelf of the closet. (*What,* Bella wondered, *is the point of buying new things if you aren't even going to look at them?*) And after the bags were put away, he was sometimes so tired, he forgot to take Bella for her walk.

Walking Bella wasn't the only thing Mr. McBride forgot. Mrs. McBride sometimes shouted at him about forgetting to take the trash out, and once refused to speak to him for a whole night after he forgot to pick her up from her doctor's appointment.

"Things have been so busy at work," he said. "And with trying to get ready for the holiday and the new—"

But Mrs. McBride slammed the door before he could finish.

🦴

One night, after the other children had gone to bed, Mrs. McBride told Mr. McBride to water the tree. "It already looks dry, and we haven't even decorated it yet," she scolded.

"I'll do it," Mr. McBride said wearily.

But Mr. McBride did *not* do it. Instead, he fell asleep on the couch.

Without taking Bella for her walk.

Bella felt sorry for Mr. McBride. Mrs. McBride would be angry with him in the morning for forgetting to water the tree, which did, in fact, look dry as a bone (though nowhere near as tasty). But she also felt very sorry for herself. Her bladder was quite full, and she didn't want to wait until morning to go to the bathroom. She would either have to wake up Mr. McBride or go on Mrs. McBride's best rug, neither of which a good girl would do.

Suddenly Bella had a much better idea.

And even though she did not like the prickly, spindly tree, and all the slamming doors and raised voices the tree had brought with it, she tiptoed quietly over and sniffed it.

It smelled like squirrel. Bella's least favorite animal. Which just went to show.

Bella was too tall to fit under the tree's branches,

but if she was very careful, she could just lift her leg high enough, as she had sometimes seen boy dogs do. She aimed for the trunk of the tree, which sat in an empty metal bowl. She couldn't help but congratulate herself. *None of the other McBride children would come up with such a good plan,* she thought. *This way, I get to go to the bathroom,* and *Mr. McBride won't be in trouble in the morning!*

Just as she was almost done, Bella felt a hard tug at her collar. Her leg was suddenly jerked away from the bowl.

"What are you doing?" shouted Mr. McBride, who must not have been quite asleep after all.

The lights flicked on, and Mrs. McBride strode in, wearing her nightgown. "Is Bella doing what I *think* she's doing?" she said. And then, her voice climbing higher, "My rug! My best rug!"

Bella looked down to see a small puddle of yellow spreading through the cream-colored threads.

"BAD BELLA!" the McBrides yelled together.

And before Bella even had time to curl her tail between her legs, Mr. McBride had scooped her up around the belly. He gave a grunt of surprise as he lifted her. In the months since Bella had arrived at the McBrides', no one had noticed how big she had grown.

Mr. McBride carried her through the kitchen into the garage.

"You stay here tonight and think about what you've done," he said, before closing the door behind him and leaving Bella alone in the dark.

TWO

The Meaning of Christmas

Bella did think about what she had done.

All night.

How did it go so wrong? I only wanted to help. That's all I ever want to do.

In the morning, Mrs. McBride let Bella out in the backyard and gave her breakfast. But she didn't speak to Bella, and she took her straight back to the garage afterward.

So Bella thought some more about what she had done.

All day.

But what, exactly, did *I do?* she wondered. She loved Mr. McBride, of course, but it seemed to her that if he hadn't pulled her away so suddenly, Mrs. McBride's rug would have been just fine.

When Mr. McBride finally opened the door to let Bella back into the house, he fixed her with a stern look. "We're giving you another chance," he said. "But you really have to behave this time."

Bella let out a sigh that fluttered through her long whiskers. When was someone going to see that she *always* behaved?

Still, she was happy to be out of the garage, which was starting to feel very damp and cold. Her stomach was rippling with hunger, but when she walked into the kitchen, her food bowl was empty. Mr. McBride must have forgotten.

Bella followed him into the living room and then stopped short at the doorway.

While she had been in the garage, the McBrides had done something to the tree. It was strung with little lights that blinked blue, yellow, and other colors Bella could not quite make out. Strings of beads were draped over the tree, as well as tiny figurines of dolls and animals and snowflakes, which glittered and winked from the branches. It was beautiful.

And there was the most delicious, buttery smell in the air.

Bella's favorite smell of all.

Popcorn.

There was popcorn strung on the tree!

"Why is Bella staring?" asked her sister. "It's like she's never seen a Christmas tree before."

"That's because she hasn't, stupid," said her brother.

"Don't call your sister stupid," said Mrs. McBride.

Bella's brother muttered something that sounded like "stupid" under his breath.

"I suppose it's a treat for Bella," said Mr. McBride, "since it's her first Christmas."

Bella's tail began to thump.

Finally she understood! Mr. McBride hadn't forgotten to feed her. And the McBrides weren't angry at her at all. They were giving her the tree as a treat. Mr. McBride had just said so himself.

They must have figured out that she was trying to help them and had finally realized what a good dog she was. They had only put her in the garage so they could surprise her with her first Christmas (whatever that was).

Perhaps, Bella thought, *"Christmas" means when someone realizes they haven't paid enough attention to someone else and arranges for a special surprise to make it up to them!*

And perhaps the tree was not so horrible after all. The popcorn had covered up the smell of squirrel, and the lights had softened its prickly bristles.

"It's dinnertime," announced Mrs. McBride, picking the baby up and leading the rest of the family to the kitchen. Bella didn't move.

"Are you staying out here to enjoy the tree?" Mr. McBride asked her.

Bella thumped her tail yes.

"All right, then," said Mr. McBride. He patted her twice on the head and gave her a little scratch behind the ears.

A scratch behind the ears! Bella couldn't remember the last time he'd done that. It felt wonderful.

After the family had gone, Bella stared at the tree for a few minutes, trying to soak up its beauty. She heard the TV in the kitchen, which she knew meant that the family was eating. Finally she padded toward the tree, looking up at all the pretty lights and sniffing its wonderful new aromas.

It wasn't just popcorn on the tree. There were striped candy sticks, too, and chocolates stuffed into shiny wrappers. Bella wasn't usually allowed to have chocolate, but regular rules probably did not count at Christmas.

Her stomach growled again, and she couldn't wait any longer. She balanced on her back paws and rested her front paws against the tree branches. She started by biting at a candy stick, which made a good appetizer.

Then she moved on to the popcorn. She savored each delicate morsel and licked the salt from her lips afterward.

It was like a game, trying to follow the fluffy trail that wound around the tree. Crisscrossing higher and higher.

Until finally, Bella had to wobble on the very tips of her toes to reach.

And then—

CRASH!

The tree toppled over.

"What in the—"

"Aaaarrgghh!"

Bella turned to see the whole McBride family standing in the kitchen doorway. Mr. McBride let out an astonished yelp, and Mrs. McBride's hand flew to her mouth. Bella's brother was laughing, but her sister had started to cry.

"Bella killed the tree!" she wailed. "Bella ruined Christmas!"

"This is the last straw!" yelled Mrs. McBride. "We can't deal with her anymore. Especially not when the little one comes."

Bella's tail curled between her legs. *What are they talking about? What's "the last straw"? What is "the little one"?*

"We never should have let your brother bring her here!" Mrs. McBride continued, turning to Mr. McBride. "He's the one who let his dog have puppies, but we're the ones stuck with this mess."

She cast an arm out at the living room—which was, in fact, a mess.

"You're right," said Mr. McBride. "I thought it would be a good idea, but—"

Bella had already stopped listening. Nothing anyone was saying made any sense anyway. Her stomach had started to churn, and she wished she hadn't eaten quite so much popcorn quite so quickly.

"Do something!" Mrs. McBride yelled over the baby, who had also begun to cry. "Do something right now!"

Mr. McBride reached for his coat and thrust his arms through its sleeves. He flung out a hand, grabbed his car keys, and then marched straight toward Bella.

Bella tried to disappear under the tree.

"Oh, no you don't," Mr. McBride said. He reached through the scratchy branches and pulled Bella out. Then he picked her up and strode back through the kitchen, past Mrs. McBride, who was trying to calm the baby.

"Where is Bella going?" her sister asked.

But nobody answered. Her brother had gone back to watching television.

"Eat your dinner," Mr. McBride said wearily. "Bella and I are going for a little trip."

Mr. McBride carried Bella into the garage, but he didn't put her down. Instead, he unlocked his car and bundled her into the back seat. Then he got in, slammed his door, and backed the car out of the garage.

Bella let out a whimper of fear.

"I'm sorry, Bella," he said. "But this is the only way. It's for the best. You'll see."

What's the only way? thought Bella. *The best for who?*

Mr. McBride punched the radio on, and they sped away into the night. Cheery lights bobbed in the yards they passed, but they did little to comfort Bella. Her heart had begun to feel very funny indeed, all strange and splintery.

Like it was starting to crack.

Three

🦴

The Pound

When Bella awoke the next morning, she kept her nose tucked neatly into her tail and her eyes tightly closed.

I wish that yesterday was just a terrible dream.

I wish that when I open my eyes, I'll be back home with the McBrides.

It was possible, wasn't it? The cold concrete underneath her could be the McBrides' garage floor. The metal clatter she heard in the distance might be Mrs. McBride preparing breakfast for everyone.

Bella allowed one eye to flutter open.

And found six eyes staring back at her.

The fur on her neck bristled as she scrambled to her feet. Three dogs watched her in silence.

One was scruffy and round with crooked whiskers. A second had droopy ears, droopy eyes, and a droopy belly. And the third was the size of a small horse.

Bella's gaze darted back and forth, taking in her surroundings.

She remembered that when Mr. McBride had left her in this awful place last night, a woman she didn't know coaxed her into a small crate and left her there for a long time. Such a long time that Bella had finally fallen asleep. It had been a very long day.

But now she was in a room that was like a big cage. It had three concrete walls and one wall that was just a chain-link gate. Beyond that, she could see more little rooms holding still more dogs.

She began to tremble. *What is this place?*

The huge horse-dog bared his huge teeth at her, and Bella let out a whimper.

"Don't worry," said the droopy-eared dog, waddling closer. "That's just Leo's smile."

The dog called Leo, who had wavy brown fur and a bite taken out of one ear, continued to bare his teeth, and Bella backed closer to the wall.

The scruffy dog padded toward Bella and circled her, his sharp ears pinned back as his sharp eyes examined her. "You don't have fleas, do you?" he asked sharply. "Because my new humans are coming to pick me up any day now, and they will not appreciate it if you give me fleas."

Bella wished she had something to hide under. She didn't really know how to talk to other dogs. Once, when she had been out for a walk with Mr. McBride, they had stopped to talk to a neighbor who was out walking his dog, too. Excited to meet a new friend, Bella had sniffed and kissed the other dog hello, but she must have done it wrong, because he'd growled and lunged at her. Frightened, Bella had turned tail and run—straight into Mr. McBride, who fell with a splash into the mud puddle behind him. After that, when they had seen other dogs, Mr. McBride had crossed the street before Bella could so much as wag her tail.

Certainly a dog had never asked her if she had *fleas*.

(She didn't, of course.)

"Where am I?" Bella asked. "Who are you? Why am I here?"

The droopy-eared dog exchanged a look with Leo. "I'm Hazel," she said. "The little guy is Runt. And this place is called the pound. It's where dogs come who are lost or alone or . . . unwanted."

Bella considered this.

She had not been brought here because she was lost. She had not come here alone. So that must mean she was—

"Unwanted?" she asked, feeling the way the strange word sat heavy on her long tongue. "What's that?"

"It means when your humans don't want you anymore," said Runt.

"It means when your humans don't *appreciate* you enough," said Hazel, stomping on one of Runt's paws with her own.

"Which is why I never want a human family," said Leo. "They don't know *how* to appreciate us."

Bella flopped down on the floor again. Was it true? Was Mr. McBride not coming back?

Am I really . . . unwanted?

"It's not true," said Bella. "It can't be!"

Hazel sighed and dropped down to the ground so that her droopy eyes were level with Bella's. Her brown ears pooled on the floor. Leo lay down, too, his tongue lolling from his mouth, while Runt paced back and forth behind them.

"Why don't you start at the beginning," said Hazel kindly.

So Bella told them about the McBrides. She told them about the other children's bad behavior, about Mr. McBride's shopping bags, and about Mrs. McBride's growing belly. She told them about being left in the garage, and about the treat tree, and about Christmas.

When she was done, Hazel and Leo shook their heads sadly. Runt was still tap-tapping around the room.

"Your problem is obvious," he barked gruffly. "Your family is having a baby."

Bella shook her head impatiently. "They already have a baby."

"*Another* baby," Runt said.

Bella didn't understand. *Why would the McBrides*

want another baby when they have four perfectly good
children already?

"How do you know?" she asked.

Hazel explained to Bella what was happening with
Mrs. McBride's belly.

As Hazel spoke, Bella had the feeling that the
droopy-eyed dog had been around a long time and seen
many things.

"If you ask me," said Leo, "the problem was that your
so-called family never wanted you in the first place."

Bella's head snapped up, her ears pinning back.
"That's not true!" she cried. "The McBrides love me. I
know they do."

Hazel shot Leo a warning look. "I'm sure you're
right," she said. "They probably didn't want to leave
you here at all. It's just because of the baby. Lots of
humans do things like this when they're expecting a
new child."

Bella thought back to what Mrs. McBride had said
the night before. *We can't deal with her anymore.*
Especially not when the little one comes.

Hazel was right. They had chosen the new baby—
the little one—over her.

Suddenly Bella had a horrible thought. "What about the other children?" she asked. "Do you think the McBrides took them to the pound, too?"

Bella didn't like it when the baby's screams woke her up in the night, chasing away her dreams of galloping through a sunny field filled with buttercups that were really made of butter. And it was never fun when her sister tied her ears up in itchy pink bows, or when her brother bonked her over the head with stuffed dinosaurs. But they all deserved to be loved.

They didn't deserve to be abandoned at the pound.

"Children don't go to the pound," said Leo. "The pound is only for dogs. And besides, humans always choose their children over their dogs."

"That's why you have to find humans with no children to adopt you," yipped Runt. "Like I did. My humans already came and picked me out. They're coming back to get me any day now. Just as soon as they get the house ready for me. Have I said?"

"But . . . ," Bella began slowly. "But I'm their child, too. I'm the best of all the McBride children."

Runt finally stopped tap-tapping. Leo's tongue

disappeared back into his mouth as he cocked his head.

"Oh, dear," Hazel breathed.

She inched closer to Bella. "Humans only have *human* children, you see. A dog can simply never be a human's child."

"But the McBrides are my parents," Bella argued.

"No, Bella," Hazel said softly. "They were your *owners*. But they aren't anymore."

Bella's thoughts began to whirl in her head. She had known, of course, that the other McBride children were different from her. She had even felt sorry for them. They couldn't reach the popcorn that fell under the couch. They had no tails to wag and only two legs to run on, and their noses barely even worked!

It had never occurred to her that *she* was the different one. The one who didn't belong.

If I don't belong with the McBrides, where do I belong?

"There's a water bowl over there," Leo said, nudging Bella gently. "Why don't you go drink a bit?"

Bella was suddenly too tired to argue anymore, so she padded over to the other side of the room. But instead of drinking, she stared down at her reflection in the bowl. She stared at her snowy fur with its black-and-brown splotches, her floppy ears, her long snout, her slick nose with its slender white whiskers.

How have I not seen it before? she thought. *I'm nobody's child. I'm just a silly dog.*

A silly, unwanted dog.

Four

The New Family

Each morning when she woke up, Bella wished with all her might that she was back at the McBrides' house.

Each morning, she opened her eyes to find that she was still at the pound.

With each morning that passed, she lost a little bit of hope. Every day, Bella felt a hole growing in her heart, much deeper than any she'd dug in the McBrides' backyard.

Leo said she shouldn't waste another thought on her humans, that they weren't worth it. *But he only knows the bad parts about them,* Bella thought.

Leo and the others had never heard about the way Mr. McBride sang silly songs on Saturday mornings while he flipped pancakes. Bella hadn't told them that in the beginning, he would even make Bella her own special pancake shaped like a doggy bone.

Leo didn't know that Mrs. McBride always smelled like honey and flowers and had skin so soft, it felt like silk when Bella nuzzled her. Or that the baby had a smile he smiled only for Bella, or that Bella's favorite game had been playing hide-and-seek with her brother and sister.

He doesn't know that before things got bad, they were really good.

Leo didn't like to talk about where he'd been before the pound. Whenever Bella asked him, he would suddenly become very interested in his breakfast, or in the game that the fluffy blond puppies in the cage across from them were playing.

But Hazel told Bella that she missed her old owner, too.

"I don't remember anything from before Lucy," she said. "She was the best owner any dog could ask for. We were together a long time. Almost forever, I think."

"So what happened?" Bella asked.

Hazel's nose twitched, and her ears seemed to droop even lower than usual. "She went to the hospital one day," Hazel said, "and never came back. The next thing I knew, our neighbor was bringing me to the pound. I've been here ever since."

Now it was Bella's turn to nuzzle Hazel, who heaved a sigh full of sadness.

Then, "It's not so bad here," Hazel said, trying to sound cheerful. "The people who take care of us are nice, and Leo and Runt are okay, too."

Runt wasn't very much older than Bella, but he had lived with four families and in two other pounds before being brought here. Some of the families had been kind at first, like the McBrides.

Some had not.

Bella understood why Runt was always tap-tap-tapping around their cage, why he startled at loud noises, and why he devoured each of his meals like he might not have another for a long, long time.

She was happy for him on the morning when his new owners came to pick him up. She had begun to wonder if they were even real.

They had just finished breakfast, and Leo had suggested a game of throw the chew toy when they heard human footsteps approaching. All the dogs in all the cages around them began to bark. All the dogs (except Leo, of course) hoped that the footsteps were coming for them.

"Here we are," said Leslie, the nice lady who took care of the dogs during the daytime. She stopped outside Bella's cage. Behind her were two men, a bit older than Mr. and Mrs. McBride. When they spotted Runt, they both smiled.

"There's our handsome little guy," said one.

The other held out a beautiful blue collar with a matching leash.

I wish I had a collar like that, Bella thought.

"Goodbye!" Runt called, after the man with the collar had fastened it around Runt's scruffy neck. Instead of attaching the leash to it, though, he scooped Runt up into his arms. "I hope you all find humans as good as mine!"

To which Leo growled.

"Goodbye, Runt!" Hazel called. "We will miss you!"

To which Leo grunted.

When darkness fell and dinner was done, the pound became a very sad place indeed. It filled with the sounds of dogs sighing, whimpering, crying. And their songs of loneliness were loudest after one of the dogs had left with a new family.

When she finally fell asleep that night, Bella had bad dreams. In them, she was frightened and running. Just when she thought she was safe, she would look up to see a dark tree, one hundred feet tall, that was about to crash down on her. As she began to run again, she heard the voices of the McBrides shouting behind her.

BAD BELLA!

When she woke up the next morning, something was different.

Instead of missing the McBrides, Bella was thinking about the look on the humans' faces when they left with Runt the day before. They seemed so happy. So loving. Bella was sure they would keep Runt forever.

Runt was no longer unwanted.

"Hazel," Bella said, as soon as Hazel had finished her morning stretches, "how did Runt find his new family?"

"At an adoption fair," said Hazel. "There should be another one coming up soon."

Bella's eyes widened, and her ears lifted as if they had been tied to balloons. She and Mr. McBride had walked by a fair once, in the field beside the school her brother and sister attended. There had been bright tents nestled between games and rides, and wonderful smells of hamburgers and ice cream wafting over the fence. Bella had wanted to go in, but Mr. McBride had tugged her away.

A fair sounded like the perfect place to find a new family!

"Do you think maybe *I* can find a new human at the fair?" Bella asked.

Hazel brushed her warm nose against Bella's. "Of course you can. All you have to do is be yourself, and some human is bound to see how special you are."

Hazel was a very wise dog, but Bella wasn't sure about this advice. After all, Hazel herself hadn't found a family to adopt her yet, had she? *And if I'm really so special,* wondered Bella, *then why did the McBrides leave me here?*

But Hazel *was* right about something. The next fair came very soon indeed.

⟡

The following day, Leslie took Bella, Hazel, and Leo to a room with a tile floor.

"It's bath time!" Leslie called. "You'll all want to look and smell your best for the adoption fair tomorrow!"

This made Bella feel a little bit happy, but mostly very sad. Because she did *not* like baths.

Neither did Leo, it turned out. When Leslie angled the hose toward him, he lunged forward and grabbed it between his teeth. Then he ran around her in circles until she was all tangled up in the hose and slipped and fell onto the soapy, sudsy floor.

Bella cringed, ready for Leslie to get up and start yelling at Leo. *That's what the McBrides would do.*

Instead, Leslie popped a soap bubble on the tip of her nose and started to laugh.

"You are one great dog," she said, shaking her own

head as she patted Leo on top of his.

Bella thought this was a very strange response.

"Why can't you behave yourself, Leo?" Hazel moaned afterward. She had stood still all through her own bath. Bella had tried to do the same, though she did run away when Leslie lifted her fluffy tail to clean underneath.

"Why should I have to get a bath? I don't want any humans to adopt me," Leo grumbled, shaking the water from his dark fur.

Later, after all the lights had been turned out and Hazel was softly snoring, Bella nudged Leo.

"Are you awake?" she asked.

"Hmm."

There was a question that had been on her mind ever since she'd met him.

"Why don't you want a family, Leo?"

"I have a family already," Leo said. "They just aren't humans."

"What are they, then?"

"Street dogs. A whole pack of them."

"But you must have had a human family sometime," Bella said.

Leo was quiet for a long moment. Bella had an awful thought.

"Did they abandon you?" she asked. "Did they leave you on the street? Is that how you met your pack?"

At least Mr. McBride brought me here, where it's warm and safe.

"No," Leo said finally, "they didn't abandon me. I ran away."

"You did *what*?"

"I lived with the same humans for four years," said Leo with a sigh. "I was like you. I thought they really loved me. Then one night I heard them talking. About how they were moving and they couldn't keep me anymore. They were going to take me to live with someone else, but I didn't want to go. I realized then that the only thing humans are good for is changing their minds and disappointing you. Why would I want to live with more of them? So when they took me for a walk, I ran away. And not long after that, I found my pack."

"Don't you miss them?" Bella asked. "Your humans?"

"No," said Leo, a little too quickly. "I like my pack

much better. Packs aren't like people. They're always there for each other. Trust me, we dogs would be a lot happier if we just kept to ourselves."

"How will you get back to your pack?"

Leo's tail thumped twice against the floor, and he smiled his sly smile. "You'll see, Bella. You'll see."

Bella stayed up long after Leo fell asleep, thinking about the adoption fair. She thought about Runt's advice to find a family with no children. This *had* worked well for Runt.

She thought of Hazel's advice about being herself. But Bella had been herself—her very best self—with the McBrides. And they had still abandoned her.

She thought of Leo, who didn't even want a human family. *Can he really be right about humans?* she wondered. *Are they all as bad as that?*

But then she thought of Leslie, heard her calling Leo "one great dog" even after he ran around and around with the hose in his mouth, and she couldn't quite believe it.

Besides, if they were happier without humans, then

why did the dogs here cry every night? If Leo was right, then why did the pound feel so very lonely?

Her thoughts circled around each other, like so many dogs chasing their own tails, until she finally fell asleep.

Five

The *Not* Fair

The next morning, before she opened her eyes, Bella wished with all her might. But it was a different wish than she had wished before.

I wish that today I will meet my new family.

She had decided not to think anymore about what Leo had said. She believed that some humans were good. All she had to do was find the right family to take her home with them.

After Bella, Hazel, and Leo had eaten their breakfasts, Leslie came in and tied colorful scraps of cloth around each of their necks.

"There!" she said. "Don't you all look nice in your bandannas?"

Bella's bandanna was blue, like the leash that Runt's new humans had brought him. Maybe it was a good sign.

"It makes you look very pretty," said Hazel kindly.

But Bella knew she would need to do more than that to get a family to believe she was special enough to take home.

Soon Leslie came in with three leashes and fixed them to the dogs' collars.

"It's time!" she sang. "Is everybody ready?"

Yes! barked Bella, which made Leslie throw back her head of curly hair and laugh.

She led them out to the yard where they were usually taken to play. Even Leo marched behind Leslie without dragging his paws. "Here we are," said Leslie cheerfully.

"But I thought we were going to the fair," Bella said, puzzled.

Hazel gave Bella an affectionate look. "This *is* the fair," she replied. "Look around!"

Bella looked. There were no tents, no rides, no games or burgers or candy. Just a few clumps of balloons strung up around the chain-link fence.

In fact, the only thing this fair had in common with the one Bella had seen before was the humans of every shape and size milling around the yard.

Lots of people looking for dogs to take home!

But there were dogs of every shape and size, too: running, playing, jumping, and yipping. All competing for attention.

Leslie took Hazel's leash off first. Hazel picked a spot in the shade and lay politely with her paws crossed one atop the other.

Bella did not think this was a very good strategy to get noticed.

Leslie took Leo's leash off next. Leo trotted around the yard and disappeared behind a tree. Bella thought this was probably so that no one would see him and think to adopt him.

Leslie took Bella's leash off last.

Bella looked around. The blond puppies who lived in the cage across from hers were all being picked up and cuddled by different people.

"They're so tiny!" cooed a woman holding one.

Bella, who was much too big to be picked up and cuddled, frowned.

"Look at this one!" called a girl, pointing her mother toward a big gray dog. "It's got the prettiest blue eyes!"

Bella's frown deepened. *What's wrong with brown eyes?* she wondered.

It seemed like every human had already chosen a dog to play with.

But nobody's choosing me.

Bella had to do something, and fast. So she took off, galloping as gracefully as she could around the yard, her tail skimming the knees of onlookers, her ears flapping in the brisk winter air. Her heart fluttered up and down in her chest like one of the little yellow butterflies she used to chase through the McBrides' backyard.

She had seen humans running with dogs in her old neighborhood. *Maybe someone here wants a dog who will run with them.*

"Look at that one!" she heard a child cry. "It's running so fast!"

Hope made Bella's heart flutter higher and her legs move faster.

"I hope it doesn't knock somebody over," replied someone else.

Bella took no notice of this, because she knew she would not.

When she grew tired of galloping, she found a toy and tossed it into the air. Then she jumped up and caught it between her teeth. This was a trick she had perfected with the fresh pairs of socks Mrs. McBride used to roll up and place in the clean laundry hamper for her to play with.

"Did you see those teeth?" asked a woman beside Bella.

"Yeah," said a man. "She looks aggressive."

Bella considered this.

She did not know what "aggressive" meant, but it sounded a lot like "impressive." Pleased with herself, she shook the toy back and forth between her teeth, then threw it up in the air again.

But the couple had moved away from her. Now they were admiring a little tiger-striped dog who, Bella knew for a fact, had never so much as caught a tennis ball in her life. The dog rolled over, and the couple squealed with pleasure. "She's doing tricks!" said the woman. "She's very talented."

Talented.

Bella knew that word. She had heard it from Mrs. McBride, whose favorite TV show was a competition where humans sang songs and people clapped for them. Mrs. McBride sometimes clapped along and said how wonderful the singers were. How *talented.*

Was *that* what humans wanted?

Bella had never tried to sing before, but it didn't look very hard. She tilted her nose up—just as the singers on the show did—opened her mouth, and tried her best to make a beautiful song come out.

"What's wrong with that dog?" she heard a voice ask. "Why is she howling like that?"

"Maybe someone stepped on her tail."

Bella let out a sigh of frustration. *I guess singing is harder than it looks,* she thought.

Then she saw something out of the corner of her eye and froze. A boy and a girl were huddled beside Hazel, taking turns petting her droopy head with their mittened hands. Their mother bent down between them.

"Is this the one you want?" she asked.

"Yes!" cried the children together.

Leslie spied the family and jogged over to them. "Hazel is one of our sweetest dogs," she said. "It's been a long time since she had anyone to look after her."

"I think we might be able to change that," said the children's mother.

"Yaaaay!" cried the children together.

Hazel's tail thumped in the dirt, but no one seemed to mind the dust cloud she was causing.

Leslie handed Hazel's new owner a thin leash.

Bella let out a whimper. She wanted to be happy for Hazel. Hazel deserved another family.

But there were hardly any humans left now.

No one's going to take me home. And I'll have to live at the pound without Hazel.

Her whimpering grew louder.

"Don't cry, Bella!" Hazel called. "Your family is coming. I know it!"

Hazel's new humans let her lead them toward Bella so that she could kiss Bella on the nose with her droopy pink tongue. Bella kissed her back.

"Any family would be lucky to have you," Hazel said.

Bella watched as Hazel's new family filled out some papers and led her to their shiny car.

"I'll miss you," she called, too late for Hazel to hear.

Then she collapsed onto the cold dirt, not caring that it would making her clean white coat look brown and filthy.

And she stayed there. Watching as other dogs were led away from the pound and into the Land of Being Wanted.

The fair was almost over.

It shouldn't even be called the fair, Bella thought miserably. *It should be called the* not *fair.*

When finally someone was interested in her, it wasn't a human at all but a large black fly that began buzzing around her head.

It buzzed.

And buzzed.

And buzzed some more.

Then it landed on her little black nose.

Finally Bella understood what "the last straw"

meant. This fly was the last straw.

She peered down at the end of her snout, where the winged culprit sat. She huffed out her mightiest huff. And when the fly tried to buzz off, she jumped up and snapped it out of midair.

And then she swallowed it.

Serves it right, thought Bella, trying to ignore the sick feeling in her stomach. Flies did not taste nearly as good as popcorn.

Suddenly she heard a woman start to laugh.

"Did you see that, Andy?" the woman said. "I think that dog just caught a fly in midair!"

"I think so, too," a man replied. "And I think she ate it!"

Bella turned to her left, where a man and woman were standing just a few feet away. They were looking at her. And they were smiling.

"You're a funny thing," said the woman, who had dark hair and hazel eyes and smelled like a bowl of fruit. She knelt down beside Bella and began to scratch behind her ears.

Bella had not been scratched behind her ears since

her last night with the McBrides. It was a most wonderful feeling.

She allowed her eyes to close and her tongue to flop from her mouth.

"I think she likes you, Alice," the man called Andy said. When Bella opened one eye, she saw that he had knelt down in front of her, too.

Mr. and Mrs. McBride would never have done such a thing. They did not like to get their clothes dirty.

Even though he was kneeling, Bella could see that Andy was tall and lean. He had crinkly eyes and smelled like french fries.

There was not a whiff of dirty diapers, or baby powder, or milk bottles.

"She's beautiful," Andy said.

"Leslie was right," the woman called Alice replied. "There's something very special about this dog. Very special indeed."

Six

🦴

The Land of Being Wanted

Bella thought she must have misheard.

What was so special about catching a fly? Any dog worth its own tail could catch a fly.

I don't think I'll ever understand humans, she thought. But she also thought it didn't matter very much why these humans had noticed her. The important thing was they liked her! *They think I'm beautiful, even though my coat is dirty. They think I'm special, even though they didn't see any of my amazing tricks!*

Leslie appeared suddenly behind Alice and Andy. She slung an arm over Alice's shoulder.

"I see you've met the Roses," she said to Bella. "They're two of my oldest friends."

Bella liked the way Leslie spoke to her like she was a human, too.

"What's her name?" Alice Rose asked.

"This is Bella," said Leslie.

"That's a perfect name for her," said Andy Rose.

Bella knew what roses were. Mrs. McBride used to cut them from the neighbor's prizewinning bushes at night and put them in a vase on the table. It made Bella happy to stare at the colorful layers of petals, to sniff their sweet, sunny smell.

Rose was the perfect name for these humans.

"I told you that you two would like her," Leslie said. "Are you thinking about taking her home?"

"I don't know," Alice said, peering into Bella's face.

Bella's heart fell. Had Alice decided that she was not so special after all?

"It depends if she wants to come home with us," Alice continued. "What do you think, Bella?"

For a moment, Bella didn't understand. Was Alice joking? *What dog wouldn't want to go home with her and Andy?*

Then, before she could stop herself, Bella lunged toward Alice and began to lap kisses all over her ears and cheeks and nose.

Yes, said her tongue. *Yes, yes, yes, yes, yes!*

Andy laughed a booming laugh. "I think that's a yes," he said.

Already these humans understood her so very well.

Leslie took a thin braided leash and fixed it to Bella's collar. Bella followed at Andy's heels as he led her toward the gate.

Andy and Alice each took a pen and a clipboard and signed a stack of papers.

Bella hoped they weren't reading them too closely. What if Mr. McBride had written somewhere that she was a Bad Bella, and her new parents decided they didn't want her after all?

No, not parents, she reminded herself. Her new *owners.*

Bella paced in nervous circles around the humans' feet until the leash was pulled tight around their legs.

She didn't mean to do it, and she tried to walk backward to untie them, but her paws didn't seem to want to move in that direction.

"I think she's claiming us," said Alice.

She and Andy laughed. Just like Leslie had laughed at Leo during bath time.

Leo!

When Alice had untangled Bella's leash, Bella looked around the yard. She couldn't see Leo anywhere. She sniffed and sniffed with all her might. But there was no trace of him in the air.

Had he been adopted without Bella noticing? Had Leslie already taken him back into the pound? Or was he still hiding somewhere, out of sight?

When Andy and Alice were done signing the papers, Leslie opened the gate for them to go.

"You'll come see me soon?" Leslie asked. "At the house?"

"Of course we will," said Alice.

"Definitely," said Andy.

Leslie leaned down and planted a kiss on Bella's head. Then Andy gave Bella's leash a gentle tug and led her out of the yard.

Bella was leaving the pound!

Although she felt very happy about this, she was a little bit sad, too.

I wish I could say goodbye to Leo.

Bella trotted behind her new humans as they walked her into the parking lot. She chanced one last glance back at the yard, hoping to catch a glimpse of Leo's big furry face.

But she did not see Leo. Instead, she noticed a hole in the fence beyond the tree she had seen him disappear behind.

Bella considered this.

"Psh!" someone hissed.

Bella turned her head to the little grove beside the parking lot.

A big furry grin peered out at her from behind one of the tree trunks.

"Why do you think she's wagging her tail?" Bella heard Alice ask.

"She's probably just so happy to be leaving the pound," Andy said.

That was true. But it was also true that she was very happy that *Leo* was leaving the pound, too.

"Good luck with your new family!" called Leo.

"I hope you find your pack!" Bella replied.

"Is there some kind of animal in those trees?" asked

Andy. "I thought I saw something move."

But Leo had already disappeared once more.

Bella followed Andy and Alice to a silver car parked at the end of the lot.

Andy opened the door for her and scooped her up to put her on the back seat. She felt nervous, remembering the last time she had ridden in a car.

Then Alice rolled Bella's window down, even though it was cold, so that she could poke her head out into the fresh air.

"Goodbye!" she called, to no one in particular, as the pound became smaller and smaller, until finally it disappeared around a bend.

As the car started to go faster, the wind rushed against Bella's nose, and she thought this must be what it was like to fly. She pretended to soar through the forests and over the fields and across the rivers.

But soaring, it turned out, was very hard work. Soon she was curled up into a neat ball on the seat, her eyes shut tight.

When Bella awoke, she heard a car door slam and wished with all her might that the Roses hadn't been a dream.

Which, as it turned out, they hadn't.

Bella peered up to see Alice opening the back-seat door. Then she helped Bella down onto the sidewalk.

Bella looked around, blinking. This place was not like any she had ever been before. It wasn't a forest, like the ones they had passed in the car. It wasn't a street with little square houses, like where the McBrides lived.

The smell of squirrels and trees had been replaced by the smell of concrete and hot cheesy pizza. A car honked, and music spilled out from a nearby window. Tall buildings rose from every street corner like silver giants.

A city, Bella thought. *That's what this place is.* She had seen such places on the McBrides' TV, but she'd never realized how very big they could be.

"Are you ready to see your new apartment?" Alice asked, patting Bella on the head.

Bella did not know what an apartment was, but she decided she was ready anyway.

Andy started to close the car door behind her.

"Uh-oh," he said. "Look at all this hair Bella shed!"

Bella lowered her tail between her legs. She knew "Uh-oh" meant she had done something wrong.

But Alice peered into the car and shrugged.

"Guess we'll have to get a lint roller," she said.

Alice led Bella in the direction of a tall building with rows and rows of windows.

"Come on, baby Bella," she said. "It's time to go home."

Bella had never been called a baby before.

Maybe the Roses were confused about the difference between dogs and children, too.

But Bella didn't mind this. Not one little bit.

Seven

The New Dog on the Block

As it turned out, Bella *did* like her new apartment.

It was smaller than the McBrides' house, but it was cozier, too.

There was no backyard. Instead, a little balcony looked out over a busy street.

Best of all, Bella still could not detect a whiff of children.

Maybe that explained why the Roses were being so kind to her, and why Alice had called her "baby." They had no children of their own. It was just as Runt had said.

The Roses poured Bella a bowlful of dinner, which she ate as politely as she could, careful not to spill crumbs on the kitchen floor.

"Look how fast she gulped it down," Andy said. "Let's fix her another bowl."

Another bowl? Bella had never had *two* bowlfuls of dinner. She backed away as Alice poured more food. What if this was a test, or a trick, like the Christmas tree had been?

"What's wrong with you, silly?" Alice asked, patting Bella's head. "Eat up."

Bella did not want Alice to think she was silly. Or that there was something wrong with her. And also, she *was* still hungry. So she ate.

That night, after the Roses climbed into bed and turned off the lights, Bella padded out to the living room to find a comfy spot to sleep. At the McBrides' house, she had always slept on the small, shabby hallway rug between the living room and the bedrooms.

"Bella?" Alice called.

A light clicked on, and Alice appeared in the doorway.

"What are you doing, funny? Come to bed!"

Bella sighed. She was trying to go to bed! *What's so funny about that?*

Still, she followed Alice into the bedroom. Then Alice patted the blanket by Andy's feet as if to signal for Bella to jump up.

But Bella would *not* jump up onto the bed.

She knew she could stay on her best behavior when she was awake. But how could she control herself when she was asleep?

What if she snored? Or made the Roses too hot? Or took up too much space?

What if I'm so nervous, I wet the bed?

Then the Roses would look at each other the way the McBrides had done when she had had her accident on Mrs. McBride's best rug.

"BAD BELLA!" they would shout.

No, sleeping on the Roses' bed was a very bad idea indeed.

Bella settled for a compromise. She found a soft spot of carpet by the bed and circled around it until she had the perfect angle. Then she settled with her nose tucked neatly into her tail and closed her eyes.

The next morning, Alice and Andy took Bella for a walk around her new neighborhood. They pointed out their favorite restaurants to her—Italian, Indian, and sushi—and visited Alice's favorite bookstore. Inside, the wooden floorboards creaked under Bella's paws, and the owner put out a bowl of water just for her while Alice browsed the shelves.

"What a sweet dog!" he said, giving her a pat. "It almost looks like she's smiling!"

Of course I'm smiling, thought Bella. *Why wouldn't I be?* Andy had told her that later that day they were going to a pet store. A whole store, just for pets!

When Alice was done in the bookstore, they walked to the park behind their apartment building. On one side, children slid down slides and swung on swings and chased each other in circles. On the other side was a green fenced area where several dogs were running after a tennis ball.

"Look!" Alice said, pointing to the dogs. "Friends for Bella!"

Andy opened the gate to the park and they walked

in, but he didn't unhook the pound leash from Bella's old collar. "Sorry, Bella," he said. "Once we've gotten you a new collar with tags, then you can run around with everyone else."

Bella didn't mind just watching. There wasn't much she would mind doing, she thought, as long as she had Andy and Alice by her side.

One of the dogs squirmed her way free from a knot of wagging tails and trotted over to Bella. She had black hair with waves of golden brown throughout, a white chest, and floppy ears. She wagged her tail as she came nearer, and Bella wagged back.

"I'm Zoey," said Zoey.

"I'm Bella," said Bella.

Zoey sniffed Bella's fur. "You smell new," she said, but not unkindly.

"I am new," said Bella. "I only got here yesterday."

"A new dog on the block!" Zoey exclaimed, wagging harder. "Did you come from the pound?"

Bella hesitated. She didn't want to admit that she had, until yesterday, been unwanted. But she was also a dog, and dogs are much more honest than humans.

"Yes," she said.

"Me too!" Zoey replied. "Almost everyone around here did."

"Really?" Bella asked, ears lifting in disbelief. She looked at the dogs running across the park, then thought of all the ones back at the pound.

There are so many, she thought. *So many unwanted dogs.*

It didn't make any sense. None of the dogs she had met since leaving the McBrides were bad. They were caring like Hazel, loyal like Leo, and friendly like Zoey. So why hadn't their humans wanted them?

"Where's your family?" Bella asked.

"Over at the playground," Zoey said. "All the ones with red hair are mine."

Bella saw two children, a boy and a girl, and a father with a baby strapped to his chest. Three children, just like the McBrides. She looked away.

"Do you like to wrestle?" Zoey asked, tugging at one of Bella's ears. "I know lots and lots of wrestling games. Come on, I'll teach you! Everyone's really friendly. You'll see!"

Before Bella could answer, Alice leaned down and ruffled the hair between Zoey's ears. "Sorry, pup," she said. "We've got somewhere to be. But Bella will be back another day."

Bella and Zoey said goodbye, and Zoey zoomed off to rejoin the game. Alice and Andy led Bella from the park. Except instead of going back to the apartment, they took her to the car. When Andy opened the back door, Bella's shoulders scrunched up around her ears. She wasn't sure she wanted to get in the car. Where would it take her?

"Don't you want to go the pet store?" Alice asked, as if reading her mind. "If you want to go, you have to get in!"

Bella wanted to go to the pet store very much, so instead of waiting for Andy to help her into the car, she jumped up onto the seat. Then she sat next to the window, patiently waiting for Alice to roll it down.

As they drove off, Bella watched the world speed by in every color she knew, and listened as the sounds of the city swirled together into a pleasant kind of hum. There were all sorts of humans on the streets. Dogs, too, and pigeons, and even a few cats.

There were no squirrels.

Bella decided she liked the city.

And she decided something else, too.

The first morning she had spent with the Roses had been the best morning of her life. She wished she could make time slow down, so that it would never have to end.

But maybe this is just the beginning, she thought. *Maybe things will only get better.*

She couldn't have known how wrong she was.

Eight

🦴

The Vet

When the car stopped and it was time to get out, Bella found herself standing in front of a small brick building. She had never seen it before, but it felt familiar somehow. She could smell other dogs nearby, and she smelled something else, too.

Fear.

Bella's tail curled between her legs. When Andy pulled on the leash, she dug her nails into the pavement. She had never been to a pet store before, but this was not what she had imagined.

"Just one more stop before the pet store," Alice said.

So where are we, then? Bella wondered. *Why have my humans brought me here?*

"Don't worry, Bella," Andy said gently. "We won't let anything bad happen to you."

Bella stood frozen another moment before she decided that if Andy said he wouldn't let anything bad happen, she believed him. And besides, she needed to be a good dog, to show the Roses that they hadn't made a mistake when they'd picked her. So she gathered up her courage and followed them into the brick building.

Inside, a tall lady with short springy hair sat behind a desk. Before she could greet them, a bright bird in a cage behind her cawed, "Take a seat! Take a seat!"

Bella's eyes widened. She had met many birds, but never one that could talk in a language she could understand.

The woman at the desk smiled. "That's Skittles, our resident loudmouth," she said, handing Alice a piece of paper to write on. "And this must be Bella. I'll let the vet know you're here.

Bella gulped. *So that's why this place feels so familiar.* She had been to see The Vet before, back when she lived with the McBrides. Back then, The Vet had worked in a different building, but it had smelled the same.

The Vet was a man who prodded your belly and held open your mouth to look at your teeth. The Vet was a man who poked you with sharp needles.

Bella hid under Andy's legs while they waited for him to come.

They won't let anything bad happen to me, she told herself. *They won't let anything bad happen to me.*

Still, when the woman at the desk stood and beckoned for Bella and the Roses to follow ("The vet will see you now!" crowed Skittles), Bella trudged along as slowly as she could, her nails click-clacking sadly against the shiny floor.

First Bella had to stand very still on a scary silver platform.

"She's a little too skinny," the woman told Alice and Andy, who listened with matching frowns. "She'll need to gain a few pounds."

Next the woman took her into a little room where Alice stroked Bella's stomach while they waited for The Vet.

"I don't think she likes this place very much," Alice said to Andy.

When the door opened again, Bella ran beneath Andy's legs once more. But when she peered up to see who had come in, it was not The Vet.

"Hi there, folks," said a new woman, one Bella didn't recognize. She had long braided hair and sparkling brown eyes. "I'm Dr. Silver, but you can call me Paula. I'll be Bella's vet today."

Bella cocked her head. Perhaps there were *two* vets. Or maybe even more!

Paula leaned down to say hello, and Bella gave her a feeble wag and a sniff. Up close, she smelled like treats.

"Ah," said Paula, "are you smelling these?"

From out of her pocket she pulled a chewy treat. She handed it to Bella, who gobbled it down in one bite.

I'm glad there is more than one vet, Bella thought. *I like this one much better than the other one.*

Feeling a bit braver now, Bella stood up for Paula to examine her. The vet felt around Bella's middle and looked at her teeth, but her hands were gentle, and she gave Bella soft pats as she worked. Then Paula gave her another treat. Bella began to relax. She thought Paula did not seem like the kind of vet who would poke her with a needle.

Once again, she was wrong.

But when Paula pulled out her needle, Andy and Alice came to sit beside Bella. Alice kissed her head while Andy scratched her neck. Bella felt two little stings above her tail, but before she could even yelp, they were gone, and Paula was handing her yet *another* treat!

"There now," she said. "Those will keep you nice and healthy, Bella. You've been a very good girl today."

Bella decided the vet was not such a terrible place after all.

(But it was not her favorite place, either.)

🦴

True to their word, Andy and Alice took Bella to the pet store next.

It was even more wonderful than Bella had imagined. There were aisles and aisles of toys and balls, and bones of every shape and size.

Andy went to buy a bag of food while Alice and

Bella picked out a round checkered bed and a doggy hairbrush.

Next they went to the toy aisle, where Alice got two packs of tennis balls, and Bella picked out a soft teddy bear like the ones the McBride children had all had. Now Bella would have one of her own!

Then she spotted the aisle with the leashes and collars. She tugged Alice toward them.

"Okay, okay," laughed Alice. "Let's get you a real leash. Which one do you like?"

Bella considered this. Leashes of every color hung in front of her like a rainbow waterfall. Some were polka-dotted, like Alice's dress. Some were striped, and others had hearts or stars or words Bella couldn't read stitched across them.

In the middle of them all was a simple blue leash, just the same color as the one Runt had gotten from his new family. And above it dangled a perfect blue collar.

They were so perfect, in fact, that Bella could have stared at them all day, but just then Andy appeared.

"The blue one," he said. "Definitely. And look what I got to match!"

Bella turned to see him holding a shiny golden tag. On it were scribbles that she was pretty sure were letters.

Letters that spell "Bella," she thought.

Best of all, the tag was shaped like a heart.

Nine

🦴

The Sky Is Falling!

Bella's first January with the Roses was also her first January ever, since she had been born in the springtime and was not yet a year old.

January was much colder than December had been, and February was colder still.

"It's freezing!" Alice yelped when she took Bella out.

"My nose is like an icicle!" Andy complained.

Bella did feel very sorry for them, because they did not have warm fur coats like she did. But she also felt happy for herself, because winter brought many wonderful things.

For instance, snow.

One morning, the Roses woke up very early and turned on the TV.

"Yes!" Alice shouted, pumping her fist into the air. "No work today!"

Bella knew enough to know that "work" was what Alice and Andy did when they were not with her.

"Work" sounded awfully boring.

Then the Roses dressed up in their snuggest coats (which were still not as warm as Bella's), even though it was so early, it was still dark out.

Andy hooked Bella's blue leash onto her blue collar, which jingle-jangled brightly with her golden name tag. Bella had to walk very softly down the hallway to the stairs, so as not to wake Mrs. Suarez, who lived next door and had very good hearing indeed.

When they got outside, Bella saw the most remarkable thing.

The sky is falling!

Except it wasn't the sky. It was fluffy white breadcrumbs, like the ones that fell from the Roses' dinner table at suppertime.

Except they weren't breadcrumbs at all. Sticking her tongue out to taste them, Bella found that the little crumbs tasted like so much more.

Like mountain streams and icebergs and the first lick of a scoop of ice cream.

Bella knew about these things because the Roses liked to watch National Geographic shows at night. And also because every evening, they gave her a tiny scoop of vanilla ice cream for dessert. ("The vet told us she needed to gain some weight!" Alice said.) Vanilla ice cream had quickly become Bella's new favorite food.

Bella's tail began to wag, and she let out a yip of happiness that made Andy and Alice laugh.

Their laughter spilled a white fog out into the dark morning.

After a while, the Roses took Bella back to the apartment and climbed into bed again.

Alice patted the covers by her feet, as she always did when she was ready to go to sleep, to invite Bella up.

But Bella had already wrapped herself into a neat ball on the round checkered bed the Roses had bought her, her head resting softly against her teddy bear.

When Bella and the Roses woke up again, the sun was high, and the world had become a cake covered in fluffy white icing.

I can't wait to sink my teeth into it! Bella thought.

The Roses took her out to the park, where they went most days now.

Zoey had been right about the other dogs who liked to play there. They were all very nice. But meeting new dogs always made Bella miss Runt, Hazel, and Leo.

Today, she was happy to see that they were the only family there.

Andy decided to invent a game.

The rules of the game were that Andy made a ball of snow and threw it straight up. Then Bella had to jump as high as she could and catch the ball in midair.

And when she caught it between her teeth and bit it into powder, she won.

Bella always won this game.

After she had won too many times to count, she noticed her paws beginning to ache. The only bad thing about snow, she supposed, was that it was cold. And the only bad thing about being a dog in the snow was that she did not have any shoes.

She tried to lift her paws one at a time so that they would warm up, but each time they sank into the snow again, they ached even worse.

"Look how Bella's walking," said Andy. "Do you think something's wrong?"

"Her paws are probably cold. We should take her back in," said Alice.

Bella sat down so that the Roses would understand that she was all right. Alice had been discussing where to build a snowman, and Bella did not want to ruin her fun. Plus, Bella was curious to see what a snowman was.

But her paws really did hurt an awful lot.

Andy fixed her leash on again, and Bella limped behind him through the snowy park.

When he turned around and saw her limping, he stopped. "This won't do," he muttered.

Then he scooped Bella up so that her head rested on his shoulder. And carried her all the way home.

When they got back to the apartment, Bella was very tired, even though it was not yet time for her afternoon nap. Snow, it turned out, was hard work.

Andy laid her on the bed. It was very comfortable.

For a moment, she almost began to fall asleep there.

Then she heard a rapid POP POP pop-pop-pop from the kitchen. She smelled something warm and buttery that made her stomach turn sour.

Before she knew it, Bella was back in the McBrides' living room, the tree crashing over her head, her little sister crying, Mr. and Mrs. McBride shouting, "BAD BELLA!"

Bella heard Alice's footsteps approaching. "Anybody want some popcorn?"

Bella shot off the Roses' bed and scampered onto her own. She curled up in her neat ball and shut her eyes tightly, pretending she was asleep.

"What's gotten into her?" Alice asked.

"I don't know," Andy replied.

Alice crouched down by Bella, holding her cold paws in her hands to warm them up. Bella cracked one eye open.

"You know we love you, don't you, Bella?" Alice whispered.

Bella did know this. The Roses told her every day. And when they were gone, the jingle-jangling of the heart-shaped tag around her neck told her for them.

Bella knew this should make her happy.

All she had ever wanted was to be loved.

But sometimes love can be scary, she thought.

What would she do if she ever lost it?

Ten

The Big News

By the time the snow was replaced with blooming flowers, Bella had forgotten to be on her best behavior *all* the time.

It was easy to forget things like that when she had so much else to think of.

Like getting belly rubs and chasing tennis balls and finding ways to avoid taking a bath.

As the weather became warmer, the Roses started spending more and more time outdoors, and they always took Bella with them.

They went on hikes in the mountains, where Bella smelled all kinds of trees and animals she had never known existed. They drove to a lake where Andy and Alice paddled in a boat while Bella watched from the shore. She kept her eyes trained on the water, ready to warn the Roses if she saw any sign of sneaky crocodiles or deadly hippos. They had watched a program on National Geographic about them, and Bella couldn't understand why Andy and Alice didn't seem at all afraid.

My humans are very brave, she thought admiringly.

Once they even went to a baseball game, where Bella and the Roses sat in a special section for humans with dogs. Bella thought baseball looked like a fun game, but she also thought it was much *more* fun to lie on the grass next to Alice and catch the peanuts Andy threw her.

Most days, though, they just walked around the neighborhood. Bella knew it very well by now, and it knew her, too. Whenever Mrs. Suarez heard Bella pass by, she came out to say hello and give her a kiss. Mr. John, who owned Andy's favorite pizza parlor, and his nephew Kevin, who worked at the register, each gave

Bella a circle of pepperoni whenever she and Andy came to pick up a pizza.

And then there were the people Bella passed on the sidewalk every day—on their way to work or coming home from school—who stopped to pet her and say what a wonderful smile she had. Bella was always smiling those days. There was so much to be happy about.

They usually ended their walks in the park, where Bella often saw her friend Zoey. Some days, they wrestled together, and other days, they dug holes. Zoey was the best digger Bella had ever met.

"Aren't you ever scared your owners will take you back to the pound?" Bella asked one day, after she and Zoey were done with their wrestling for the afternoon. Zoey's owners were standing at the edge of the park, talking to Alice and Andy while their children played in the playground.

"No," said Zoey simply. "My family loves me too much to leave me."

"But they have children to take care of. And besides," Bella said, repeating what Leo had told her, "humans always choose their children over their dogs."

"But the children are my best friends," said Zoey. "They would never let my mom and dad abandon me, even if they tried. Which they won't."

Bella considered this.

Zoey chased her tail in circles until she fell over.

Bella thought about Hazel, who had also been adopted by a family with children, and hoped that she was all right.

"ACHOO!"

Zoey's sneeze was so enormous that it caused Bella to leap into the air in surprise.

Zoey had sniffed too hard at a patch of daffodils, and her nose was covered in yellow dust.

Bella sighed as she watched Zoey try to wipe the dust off her nose with her paws. She hoped Zoey was right and that her family would always take care of her. *Zoey would never make it on her own.*

One morning, the Roses led Bella out to the car. Even though Bella trusted the Roses, she always got a nervous feeling in her belly when they took her driving. But they were usually very good about telling her where they were going.

"We're going to see a special friend of yours!" Alice announced today.

"It'll be a great day for all of us," Andy added.

Andy took Alice's hand and kissed her on the cheek.

Once she knew where they were going, Bella usually focused on getting her head as far out the window as she could. Today, though, she was busy wondering who the special friend could be. All her friends lived here, in the neighborhood. Except, of course, for Runt, Hazel, and Leo. But the Roses didn't know about them.

They took a short drive toward the edge of the city and slowed in front of a little blue house with a white picket fence around the yard.

A woman waved from the porch, and as Andy pulled into the driveway, Bella saw who it was.

Leslie.

Bella pinned back her ears and began to tremble as Leslie walked toward the car. Were the Roses leaving her here?

Is Leslie taking me back to the pound?

"Don't worry," Alice said, ruffling Bella's ears. "No one is going to take you back to the pound."

Bella felt herself relax. She liked how Alice so often seemed to know exactly what she was thinking.

"Hello, Bella!" Leslie called. She bent down, kissed Bella's nose, and rubbed behind her ears in just the right place. Then she hugged Andy and Alice.

"Come in, come in," she said, leading them through the door.

The Roses sat down on a green sofa in the living room. Then Leslie opened the back door so that Bella could play outside and also do some very important business in the backyard, which was surrounded by the picket fence. The grass was covered with white flower petals that rained down in a soft shower from a tree above. There were interesting bugs to chase in the pretty flower beds and even a few sticks that were the perfect size to gnaw on.

As she sniffed a particularly smelly plant, Bella heard a great whistling sound nearby and ran to the back of the yard. She poked her head between two loose pickets in time to see a train trundling by across a field. Bella watched until it was out of sight, wondering where it was going, before turning her attention to chasing after a fat cricket.

When she was tired of playing, she trotted back inside.

Leslie was holding Alice in a tight embrace, and Andy stood behind them, a huge grin on his face.

"I'm so happy for you!" Leslie said. "I have to start knitting little hats and scarves!"

Bella looked from Leslie to Alice and Andy.

"Bella must be very happy, too!" said Leslie.

"What do you say, Bella?" asked Andy. "Does our big news make you happy?"

Bella could tell that the right answer was yes, so she thumped her tail.

She wondered briefly *why* everyone was so happy, but she knew that sometimes humans got excited about strange things, like boring TV shows with no animals in them or getting a new vacuum cleaner, and it really was past her nap time already. She found a sunny spot on Leslie's carpet and circled around it until she plopped down in the perfect place. She fell instantly asleep.

As she slept, she dreamed of Leslie wrapping colorful scarves around her neck and taking her out to play in a snowstorm of flower petals. Zoey and Leo were there as well, jumping up and down and chasing one another through the white blossom blanket as a train whistled in the background.

When Alice woke her up to go home, Bella wasn't altogether sure she hadn't dreamed the entire afternoon.

Eleven

The Nursery

As the days grew longer, Bella became even more contented with her new family.

Andy took Bella for long runs each morning, before the sun became too hot. Once or twice, Bella even let Alice coax her onto the foot of the bed for her after-running nap, though she still always slept on her own bed at night.

Bella found that she thought less and less of the McBrides, though she still sometimes dreamed of a giant tree toppling down on her, and hearing their voices yell out "BAD BELLA!"

It was just a nightmare, she would tell herself in the morning. *You live with the Roses now, and everything is wonderful.*

One day, when the sun was just beginning to set, Andy took Bella out to the park to play. Zoey was nowhere to be seen, and neither were any other dogs. The only other people there were two children throwing a Frisbee back and forth.

Luckily, Andy had brought a tennis ball.

"Ready, girl?" he said. "Go get it!"

The tennis ball soared from his hand to the far corner of the park.

Bella pumped her legs as hard as she could and flew after the ball.

When she ran like that, she was sure she was the fastest dog who had ever lived. Faster, even, than the wind.

But when she got to the fence, there was no ball to be found.

There was, however, a hole in the chain link.

Bella's heart sank. If her ball had rolled through it, she couldn't bring it back to Andy. Going outside the fence on her own was against the rules.

"Looking for this?" called a gruff voice.

Except it sounded like "Ookinordis?"

A huge shadow stepped out from behind a tree on the other side of the chain-link fence.

Leo!

Her old friend wagged his tail. He dropped Bella's tennis ball from his mouth and grinned.

Bella stepped closer to the fence so that she could kiss him hello.

"Leo!" she cried. "What are you doing here?"

"I move around a lot," Leo said. "My whole pack does. Otherwise, the dogcatchers will find us and take us to the pound. What are *you* doing here?"

"I'm with one of my new humans," Bella replied. "He's on the other side of the park."

Bella looked over her shoulder. Andy was standing with a hand on his hip, looking curiously at her.

"How are you?" Bella asked.

"Great!" Leo said.

Bella considered this. Leo did not, in fact, look very good at all. He had a long scratch across one of his cheeks, and his left eye was swollen. He was so skinny, she could see the shape of his ribs through his fur.

And he smells like a dumpster.

Bella did not say this, of course. She wouldn't want to hurt Leo's feelings.

"Bella!" Andy called. "What are you doing over there? Come, girl!"

Bella didn't like ignoring Andy, but she suddenly had a very good idea indeed.

"Leo," she said, "my humans and I live in that tall building over there. Why don't you come back with me to meet Andy? I'm sure he would take you home with us."

Leo's face scrunched up, like he had just been bitten by a flea. "I'm glad you're happy, Bella," he said, "but you know I don't do humans."

"But they have ice cream and tennis balls and National Geographic! And I'm sure they would love you."

Leo shook his head. "No thanks."

"Well, hi there, buddy," said Andy. Bella turned around to see that he had crossed the park and was standing close behind her, staring at Leo.

"Gotta go!" yipped Leo. "See you around!"

Leo galloped off before Andy could even hold his hand out to be sniffed.

"Stay here, Bella," said Andy. Then he ran to the nearest gate and out onto the street. He looked both ways for any sign of the big, skinny dog.

But, as usual, Leo had already disappeared.

As it turned out, the Roses might not have had time to take care of another dog anyway.

Even when they weren't at work, they started keeping themselves busy doing things around the apartment.

First Alice cleaned out her study. Andy painted it yellow, and then he and Alice slowly filled it with boxes. Bella did not know what was in the boxes. She was not allowed inside the yellow room.

"I don't want you breathing those paint fumes," Alice explained. "And there are too many tools and sharp things in there right now. You could hurt yourself. Besides, this way, the nursery will be a surprise."

Bella felt a little curious to know what the nursery was. But she also felt quite grumpy. When the Roses were working in the nursery, they couldn't be with her.

And for the first time in a long while, she was beginning to feel afraid again. Some nights, she lay awake, puzzling and worrying about the way things seemed to be changing.

The McBrides' last "surprise" for me ended with a trip to the pound, she thought.

Bella was not fond of surprises. Not at all.

Twelve

The Awful Truth

As the days grew cool again and the leaves turned crimson and gold, things in the apartment went from bad to worse.

Andy and Alice seemed busier than ever. They never forgot to take Bella for her walks, or feed her breakfast and dinner, or even kiss her on the head at bedtime and tell her they loved her.

But even so, things were different.

She often heard the Roses talking about their savings account and about how Alice was feeling. Andy helped Alice up off the sofa, even though she seemed perfectly capable of helping herself up. And when they walked down the stairs, Andy held her arm as if he were afraid she might fall. Bella had even heard them talking about the hospital, and this made her feel very worried indeed.

Bella knew that the hospital was where you went to see a doctor—a kind of vet for humans. She remembered Hazel's story, about how her human went to the hospital one day and never came back. She quivered to think of Alice having to go there.

One misty morning, while Alice stayed in bed, Andy walked Bella over to the park. When they got there, Zoey was already waiting.

"Wanna play wrestling?" she asked, wagging her tail and swiping a playful paw at Bella.

Bella flopped onto her belly instead.

"What's wrong?"

"I don't know," said Bella. "I think one of my humans is sick."

"Oh no, oh no, oh no, oh no!" cried Zoey, zooming in a nervous circle. "What's wrong with her?"

Bella told Zoey about Andy and Alice's strange behavior. To her surprise, when she finished, Zoey switched directions and gave a joyful yip as she turned and began to circle the other way—a happy circle.

"What's wrong with you?" said Bella. "My human could be sick!"

"I'm sorry, Bella," said Zoey. "But she's not sick. It's so exciting!"

"What is?!" Bella cried. She was so very tired of not knowing what was going on.

"Your humans are having a child!" Zoey exclaimed.

"What."

"A child! A baby!"

"No."

No, no, no. It can't be true, can it?

"Yes! A nursery is a place to keep a baby. And Andy just wants to make sure Alice and the baby are healthy."

If Bella had not already flopped down on the ground, she would have thrown herself there now. She began to tremble, and she buried her face in her paws. Leo's voice echoed in her head. *Humans always choose their children over their dogs.*

That's why you have to find humans with no

children to adopt you, Runt had yipped.

Then it was Hazel she heard, the voice gentle and kind, but the words so cruel. *A dog can simply never be a human's child.*

"Bella? What's wrong?" Zoey asked.

Dogs do not cry with tears like humans do, but a lump stuck in the back of Bella's throat all the same. She let out a small whimper.

"What's wrong?" Zoey repeated, nuzzling Bella.

"*You're* wrong!" Bella growled. "They aren't having a child. They wouldn't do that to me!"

"But Bella, they aren't going to—"

Before Zoey could finish, Bella heard Andy calling her.

"Bella! Time to go. Sorry girl, but I have a busy day today!"

Bella turned her back on Zoey and trudged toward Andy.

"Bye, Bella!" Zoey barked cheerfully. "Congratulations!"

Bella was too angry to say goodbye.

When Bella and Andy got home, Alice was standing in the kitchen, where something sizzled on the stovetop.

"I'm making an omelet," she said when they came in. "Anybody want a bite? I put some extra butter in today."

Bella accidentally inhaled a big gulp of hot buttery air. It smelled for all the world like . . . popcorn. She felt a sudden tug in her stomach, like she was going to be sick.

"Is Bella okay?" Alice asked.

Before she could stop herself, Bella felt her breakfast in her throat, and soon it was lying in a puddle on the kitchen floor.

When she saw what she had done, Bella dashed into the bedroom and threw herself under the Roses' bed. She knew what was coming. The Roses would be upset at her for dirtying their floor and ruining their morning.

She waited to hear them yell, "BAD BELLA!"

Or maybe even, "VERY BAD BELLA!"

But there were only low voices talking in the kitchen. After a few minutes, she heard footsteps coming into the bedroom.

"Bella?" Alice called.

"Where is she?" asked Andy.

"I don't know," said Alice, her voice climbing with worry.

Then Andy's head appeared beside Bella's. "You'd better come look."

Alice's head appeared, too. "Why is she curled in a ball like that?" she asked. "What's wrong?"

"Should we take her to the vet?"

Nothing is wrong! Bella wanted to tell them. *It was just Zoey stuffing silly ideas into my head. And the smell of extra butter makes me feel sad and scared and angry all at once. And I do* not *want to go to the vet, even if there is a talking bird and even if Paula does give me lots of treats. I just want to go back to the way things used to be!*

But Bella did not know how to say all these things, so instead she uncurled herself a little, lifted her snout from the floor, and licked Andy's palm.

"She seems better now," he said. He reached under the bed and took hold of Bella's shoulders where they met her chest. Then he gently pulled her out.

Alice looked her over and stroked Bella's tummy. "She should lie down up here," she said to Andy, patting the pillows. "Where it's comfortable."

Andy helped Alice to her feet. Bella looked up. For the first time, she noticed that Alice's stomach seemed bigger than usual. Just like Mrs. McBride's stomach had before the tree arrived.

Bella let out a low moan.

"Can you get her onto the bed?" Alice asked Andy.

But no matter how they tried to convince her, Bella would not move from her spot on the carpet. Not even when Alice brought her a large scoop of vanilla ice cream.

As winter drew closer, the days grew darker, and so did Bella's moods. Zoey had been right after all. Bella knew the awful truth now.

Alice and Andy are going to have a child.

Alice's stomach got rounder each day, just as Mrs. McBride's had. Andy's face looked more and more tired, just like Mr. McBride's had. The only difference was that Bella understood what was happening this time.

And the other only difference was that the Roses

were still pretending like nothing was going to change. They still petted Bella and kissed her on the head and threw her tennis ball.

But that's the way it had started with the McBrides, too.

It's only a matter of time before everything changes, Bella thought.

And this time she was right.

Thirteen

The Tree Returns

One morning, Bella awoke to find lacy frost covering the grass. Little white puffs huffed from her nose when she and Andy went for their walk together.

"You have to take care of Alice today," Andy said. "Keep an eye on her while I'm gone."

Bella wondered where he was going without them. It was Saturday, which usually meant that Andy didn't have to go to work. Probably he had to do something related to the baby. Everything was about the baby nowadays.

Leslie had even thrown the baby a party, which Bella thought was very silly, considering that the baby had not even been born yet. And especially considering that no one had ever thrown Bella a party.

Alice had finally let her see the nursery, which was covered in fluffy toys and soft blankets and bright colors. It was the most beautiful room Bella had ever seen, which made her feel very sad, because none of it was for her.

Andy and Alice had signed up for parenting classes, which meant Bella had to stay alone in the apartment every Thursday evening. Even though she did not like being left by herself, she remained on her best behavior. She did not eat the snacks the Roses left out on the counter or go exploring in the trash can.

It was very important for Bella to be on her best behavior.

Then maybe, just maybe, Andy and Alice will still want me when the baby comes.

Andy was gone all afternoon. Bella tried her best to take care of Alice while he was away. She wished that

Alice would lie down and rest, but her human spent the whole day cleaning instead. First she scrubbed the dishes and wiped the counters. Then she moved the sofa and chairs and swept underneath them.

Alice did not usually like to clean. In fact, Bella had never seen her clean so much.

She followed Alice from room to room and corner to corner, keeping an eye on her, until finally Alice plopped down on the sofa.

"Do you want to come sit on the couch?" she asked Bella.

Bella much preferred to lie underneath the coffee table, where she could see Alice without disturbing her.

Alice gave a long sigh. Then she picked up the phone.

Keeping an eye on someone was very hard work, and Bella had begun to feel sleepy.

She allowed herself to close her eyes for just a few seconds.

When she opened them again, Alice was still lying on the couch, deep in conversation.

"I just don't think she's happy here," she said.

She paused to listen to something on the other end.

Bella shut her eyes again so that Alice would think she was still asleep.

"All she does is mope around and hide under the furniture. She's not the dog we know anymore."

Bella's toenails dug into the carpet. *Alice is talking about me!*

"You're right," Alice said. "I don't think we can avoid it any longer. We're going to have to take her in."

In? In where? Bella thought frantically.

"No, not today. But soon. Before the little one comes. I know it's her least favorite place in the world, but it's best for her in the long run."

Another pause.

"I hope so, too. It breaks my heart."

Bella heard a jangling at the door.

"Leslie? Andy is home. Yes, with the tree."

The tree? Andy is bringing home a tree?

"Thanks for the advice. Yes, Bella will see you soon."

Alice's words buzzed like bees. And each one stung.

Leslie will see me soon? Before the little one comes? They're taking me to my least favorite place in the world?

But that must mean . . .

They were taking her back to the pound.

~

Everything was just as it had been a year ago.

Bella watched helplessly as Andy put the tree up in the middle of the living room. A spindly, prickly, seasick-green tree that stank of squirrels. Alice, who seemed not to notice the smell or mind the prickles, waddled around it, stringing it with lights.

"Isn't it beautiful?" Alice asked Bella. "Isn't this just going to be the most wonderful Christmas ever?"

But Bella was not fooled.

When she had spied the McBrides' decorated tree for the first time, Bella had thought Christmas was when someone realized they hadn't paid enough attention to someone else and arranged for a special surprise to make it up to them.

But now Bella knew what Christmas meant. It meant she was once again unwanted.

She lay against the cold kitchen floor while the Roses decorated the tree and hummed cheerful songs. Was it really so easy for them to be happy, knowing they were going to abandon her?

Suddenly a memory came to her. Lying on a different cold floor, listening to Leo tell his story.

I lived with the same humans for four years. I was like you. I thought they really loved me. Then one night I heard them talking. About how they were moving and they couldn't keep me anymore. They were going to take me to live with someone else, but I didn't want to go.

Bella didn't want to go, either.

I realized then that the only thing humans are good for is changing their minds and disappointing you. Why would I want to live with more of them? So when they took me for a walk, I ran away. And not long after that, I found my pack.

Bella hadn't wanted to believe Leo then, but maybe he was right after all. She couldn't face the idea of returning to the pound, only to go home with a different set of humans who would make her love them only to leave her again. She just couldn't. She wouldn't.

Packs aren't like people. They're always there for each other. Trust me, we dogs would be a lot happier if we just kept to ourselves.

Bella had made up her mind.

She would run away and find Leo's pack. Maybe they wouldn't have vanilla ice cream and tennis balls and National Geographic, but they also wouldn't abandon her. They would be loyal.

She started to think up a plan.

I'll go back to the corner of the park where I saw Leo in the summer, Bella thought. *Maybe he comes there a lot, and I can pick up his scent and follow it. Or maybe I can wait until he comes back.*

And then Leo would take her to his pack, and they would surely want her. They would be her family forever.

Bella would run away the first chance she got.

Fourteen

The Escape

Bella's chance came sooner than she expected. Much, much sooner, in fact.

When Alice and Andy had finished decorating the tree, Andy swept up all the loose pine needles into a garbage bag.

"I'm just going to take this down to the trash," he said.

When Andy took the trash out, he usually took Bella with him. And he didn't put her on her leash, because she waited inside the lobby door while he swung the trash into the dumpster. She wasn't allowed outside without her leash. That was the rule.

Bella felt like her heart was a rope toy in a tug-of-war contest at the park. *I wish I could have just one more night with Andy and Alice.* For even now, she still loved them. But who knew when they might try to take her to the pound? Maybe even tomorrow. *This might be my only chance to run.*

Making up her mind, Bella scrambled to her feet and stood by the door while Andy slid his shoes on.

"Of course you can come," he told her.

A not so very small part of Bella had hoped that Andy would decide to go without her.

She glanced around her apartment. One last look at her round checkered bed, at her soft teddy bear, at her basket of tennis balls and her perfect blue leash.

One last look at Alice, who was staring up at the tree with a smile on her face. The twinkling lights made her smile shimmer and her cheeks glow. She was even more beautiful than the golden angel that looked down from atop the tree.

Bella had never felt so sorry in her entire life.

"Are you coming?" Andy asked.

Bella forced her gaze away from Alice. Andy was already holding the door open. Reluctantly she followed him out and into the hallway.

For the last time, she followed him past Mrs. Suarez's apartment, down the stairs, and into the little lobby where she usually waited. For the last time, she watched as Andy opened the door with the strong, gentle hands that had petted her and scooped her up and held her leash.

She would miss those hands.

She would miss everything about her humans.

But the moment had come.

It's now or never.

As soon as Andy opened the door wide enough, Bella darted past him and skidded out into the darkness.

She heard him call after her, heard his shoes slapping against the pavement, but it was too late.

Bella had already sped away into the night.

🦴

Bella tore down the street to the park, which was empty. She followed the chain-link fence to the place where she had met Leo.

It was a shivery-cold night, and a dark one, too. Bella could smell something wet and familiar hanging in the air, but she didn't have time to consider what it was.

When she reached the corner where she had seen Leo, she stopped and lowered her nose to the dry grass. She sniffed with all her might and hoped with all her heart. But neither worked. She couldn't smell Leo anywhere.

She circled the spot, over and again. She tried big circles and small circles, and even figure-eight circles. But there was no trace of Leo.

She began to shake.

Perhaps if she howled her mightiest howl, he would hear it and come save her.

Then again, if she howled her mightiest howl, Andy would *definitely* hear her. He would come find her, put her in the car, and perhaps even take her straight to the pound.

Something cold and wet landed on Bella's nose. She licked it.

Snow. That's what she had smelled in the air.

Snow was great fun when Bella had her humans to

play with. But what would happen if it kept snowing and snowing until the ground was covered? *My paws will be cold, and there will be no Andy to carry me inside.*

What did Leo and his pack do when it snowed? Where did they go?

Only then did Bella remember what Leo had said about the dogcatchers. *My pack has to keep moving. Otherwise, the dogcatchers will find us and take us to the pound.*

That meant Leo and his pack would be long gone by now. She would never be able to follow their trail from here.

Bella had run away to find Leo, but now she had no way of tracing him. Either Andy would find her and take her to the pound or the dogcatchers would.

It was hopeless.

Just then, she heard her name being called out.

"Bella!" yelled Andy.

"Bella!" cried Alice.

She whipped her head toward the busy street. Andy was running down the sidewalk, Alice following behind him.

"Stay there, Bella!" Alice demanded.

Panic welled up in Bella's heart like a bathtub filling with water. She wanted nothing more than to run straight into Alice's arms.

But I can't go back to the pound.

She did the only thing she could think to do.

She took off toward the busy street, just as the cars were all coming to a stop. She leaped across the sidewalk in one bound.

"Stop, Bella!" she heard Andy yell.

And then she heard his and Alice's voices together. "BAD BELLA!" they shouted.

The words hurt much worse than any vet's needles, but Bella did not stop. She did not stop when she heard car horns honking at her, either. She galloped across the street and reached the other side just as the cars began moving again, preventing Alice and Andy from following her. She sped down a block, then two, three, four. Past Alice's favorite Indian restaurant and Mr. John's pizza shop. Past the brightly lit shops and the groups of people with their shopping bags. She ran until she lost count of the blocks, until she wasn't sure what direction she was running in anymore.

As she ran, her heart-shaped collar jingle-jangled. It sounded like the voice of someone laughing at her. And no matter how fast she galloped, she couldn't outrun it.

Foolish Bella, laughed the voice, *thinking the Roses would keep you forever. You're just a silly, unwanted dog.*

Finally Bella stopped when she saw something familiar up ahead. It was the bookstore Alice liked, the one whose nice owner had let Bella come inside on her first morning with the Roses.

Will he let me come inside now?

But the lights were all off in the store.

It did, however, have a dark, covered doorstep that would shelter Bella from the snow and hide her from the dogcatchers. The snow was falling faster now, and Bella's coat was wet and heavy.

She stepped up onto the doorstep and circled around and around, trying to find the softest spot on the concrete.

Except there was no soft spot. No teddy bear to use as a pillow.

Finally Bella slumped onto the hard step and curled

in the tightest ball she could, tucking her nose neatly into her tail.

Though she was sure that Alice and Andy weren't following her anymore, Bella heard their voices over and over again. "*BAD BELLA!*" they shouted.

She had tried her very hardest to be a good dog. To be good enough for a human family to love. And she had failed.

A group of girls broke into song across the street. A man on the next block whistled for a cab. Somewhere in the distance, a siren began to blare.

Bella squeezed her eyes shut.

If I can't be a good dog, she thought, *I'll just have to try to be an invisible one.*

Fifteen

The Park at Night

Although it was already morning when Bella awoke, everything was silent and still.

Snow covered the ground, like the world had been tucked underneath a fluffy white blanket.

It would have been beautiful if it hadn't been so cold. And if she had someone to play snowballs with her and to carry her home when her paws began to ache.

But Bella was all alone.

The dogcatchers would surely be looking for her soon. Alice and Andy would have called them by now.

Her stomach gave a loud rumble. She had not eaten dinner the night before. How was she supposed to find food, now that she was on her own?

I wish Leo was here, she thought. *He would know.*

She couldn't stay in the bookshop doorway. The owner would probably arrive soon to open the shop, and he might recognize her. Bella stood up and stretched her cold muscles. She looked left. She looked right. She was so used to the gentle tug of her leash showing her the way, but now she did not know which direction to go.

Right, she thought, would take her back toward the Roses' apartment, so finally she chose left. Away down the sidewalk she trotted, keeping close to the buildings. She wished she didn't have so many splotches of black and brown. They stood out in the bright snow, making her easy to see.

But luckily for Bella, there weren't many people to hide from. The streets were oddly empty of cars and buses, and there were very few footprints in the snow. People were bundled up in their warm houses with their happy families.

The thought made Bella ache with loneliness.

She walked on for a long time—to where, she didn't know. She kept her nose to the ground, sniffing for any sign of Leo. But all she smelled were indoor dogs—a poodle who had just come back from the groomer, and a golden retriever who had been for a swim somewhere stinky. Dogs who were wanted.

Just as she was starting to feel weak with hunger, a new smell made her nose twitch.

It wasn't a dog smell. It was a food smell. Not a very good one, but still . . . Bella followed its trail to a garbage bag that someone had left on the curb.

Without opening it, she knew that inside there was a banana peel, an empty potato chip bag, candy bar wrappers, and a bunch of broccoli that had gone bad. There was something else, too. Something cheesy. The crust of a grilled cheese sandwich, perhaps?

Whatever it is, Bella thought, *it'll have to do.*

Glancing over her shoulder to make sure no one was watching, she tore the bag open with her teeth. Its contents spilled out onto the street, and she began to nose through them until she found a few mouthfuls of macaroni and cheese that had stuck together. She ate them quickly, partly because she was so hungry, and partly because macaroni and cheese does *not* taste good when it is cold.

Just as she swallowed down the last bite, she heard a voice.

"Hey! Look at that dog!"

Bella's head whipped around to see a girl standing in the open doorway of the house behind her.

"It's eating from the trash!"

A woman appeared beside the girl and frowned. "Is it by itself? Here, doggy!"

The woman had a plate in her hands, and now she held it out in Bella's direction. The smell of turkey and cheese—warm and melted this time—floated toward Bella.

She took a step toward the house. In the back of her mind, she knew she should be careful, but all she could think about was how empty her stomach was. How good the sandwich would taste on her tongue.

"That's right," the woman coaxed. "Here, doggy."

The woman came slowly down the stairs, the smell of the sandwich growing stronger with every step she took, until finally she stood in front of Bella on the sidewalk. Bella's stomach rumbled again. One more step, and she could reach the sandwich.

She lifted a front paw—

—and suddenly the woman's free hand shot out, gripping Bella's collar.

It was a trap!

Bella tugged and twisted, causing the woman to lose her balance. The plate went crashing to the ground as Bella finally shook free. Taking one last look at the turkey and cheese sandwich, as if just the sight of it might be enough to fill her belly, Bella turned away and broke into a gallop. The woman and the girl were both shouting behind her—"Wait! Come here, doggy!"—but Bella did not so much as cast them a backward glance.

She ran and ran until she came to a part of the city she didn't know, which was just as well, because no one here would know her, either. When she couldn't run anymore, she walked and walked, ducking out of sight whenever she passed a human. But the city was filled with humans. And when the snow melted, they would fill the sidewalks and streets again. She had already almost been caught once. How long could she last on her own before one of them trapped her again?

🦴

It was as daylight was starting to fade that Bella saw a big park across the street, and, for the first time in many hours, her ears perked up. Parks were full of places to hide.

Then, as she was looking both ways before she crossed, she caught sight of a flyer on the nearest lamppost.

Bella froze midstride, one paw hovering in the air as she stared. Her heart began to thump as she considered what was on the paper.

It was a picture. Of *her*! On the lamppost! With lots of big, bold letters underneath.

The picture had been taken the day she and the Roses had gone to watch the baseball game. The baseball field stretched out behind Bella, and the sunset behind the baseball field. Bella looked up at her own smiling face, her pink tongue poking out just slightly from her mouth. When this picture was taken, Bella had been filled to the brim with boiled peanuts and happiness.

But now she felt only sadness and fear.

Bella thought suddenly of a movie she had once seen with Andy and Alice in which the police hung posters like this one to try to find escaped criminals.

Is that what I am now? A criminal?

The thought of Andy and Alice reporting her to the police made Bella want to howl with sorrow.

But there was no time for that. If the police were really looking for her, she would need to find a very good hiding spot indeed. *If only I was as good as Leo at disappearing!*

Bella raced across the street to the park and ran for the trees. She kept going until she was surrounded by them and decided she must be in a forest.

In the forest, the ground was not so snowy and cold, and Bella spotted a tree with big roots that she could curl up between. She lay down and found that there was even a soft layer of leaves beneath her. It was nothing like her bed at home, but it was better than the concrete of the bookshop doorstep.

Bella looked around, thinking that if she couldn't find Leo's pack, maybe living in the forest wouldn't be so terrible. Maybe there was even a wolf pack in the forest, like the ones from National Geographic, who would take Bella in.

Except that wolves frightened Bella.

And that as the darkness fell and she closed her eyes, she began to hear strange noises that frightened her, too.

Snap!

Creak!

Thump!

Bella was too afraid to open her eyes but too afraid to fall asleep, either.

Finally she heard a loud *whoosh* above her head and cracked one eye open. She found two eyes staring down at her.

"Who?" asked the bird on the branch above her.

Bella remembered Skittles, the talking bird at Paula the vet's office. But this bird did not look like Skittles. It was rounder, with gray and silver feathers and enormous yellow eyes. It obviously knew how to speak, though. Perhaps all birds knew how to speak, if they chose. Perhaps this bird would help Bella settle into the forest—show her where to find food and water. Perhaps they even could be friends!

For the first time since leaving the Roses' apartment, Bella felt a flicker of hope.

"I'm Bella," she said eagerly, lifting herself up to stand. "Who are you?"

The bird ruffled its wings. "WHO!" it said again, louder this time, and now its yellow eyes began to glitter in a way that frightened Bella.

"I'm . . . Bella," she said again, though this time the words came out as a whimper.

The bird unfolded its giant wings and flapped off its branch. "WHO!" it screeched, swooping down toward Bella. "WHO! WHO! WHO!"

Except now Bella understood that even though it said "WHO," what it meant was "Go away! Or else. . . ."

Bell let out a yelp and began to run the way she had come, weaving through the trees until she found herself back in the open park. She was so frightened that she streaked across the snow-covered grass without paying much attention to where she was going at all, until suddenly her paws were slipping and sliding out from under her. She looked down to see that she had stepped onto a large oval of smooth ice.

And in the middle of the oval, rising up in front of her, was a tree. A spindly, prickly, seasick-green tree.

The tree was at least a hundred feet tall.

Its branches were covered in colorful lights that glared down at her like the eyes of the bird in the forest, only this time there seemed to be thousands of them. Atop the very highest branch was a huge blazing star.

It's the giant tree! The one from my nightmares!

Her heart thumping wildly in her chest, Bella turned tail and ran once more, skidding across the ice before the tree could topple over her, like it did in her dreams. Finally she felt her paws reach snowy ground. When she looked back, panting, the tree was far behind her. She was safe, for now.

But she was also running out of places to run.

Sixteen

The Little Blue House

Bella awoke the next morning underneath an alleyway dumpster, where she had finally curled up the night before.

She was hungry, and cold, and still tired.

It took her a moment to realize that a sound had woken her up. A loud whistling and a low rumble that seemed to make the ground shake.

Where have I heard that sound before? she wondered.

Then, with a jolt, she remembered—she had heard

the sound at Leslie's house. It was a train whistling past.

The sound gave Bella an idea. It was not a marvelous idea, or even a very good one.

But it was the only one she had left.

꒰ꙮ꒱

Bella found her way to the train tracks and began walking in what she hoped was the right direction. She walked for a long time, until her paws were so cold that she began to limp. She felt as if tiny icy hands were pinching her all over.

Just when she was sure she had followed the train tracks in the wrong direction, she spotted the back of the little blue house peeking up above the white picket fence.

Bella left the tracks and forced herself to trot toward Leslie's house. She planned to bark until Leslie came to the door. Surely Leslie would let her warm up and give her food before calling the Roses or taking her to the pound.

Then Bella would ask to go out in the backyard. She remembered there had been two loose pickets in the fence. She had poked her head between them to watch the train roll by. Now she would be able to escape through them before Leslie could stop her.

And then . . . well, she would think about *then* when she had food in her belly.

Bella stole between the Leslie's house and the one next to it, coming to a stop by the front gate of the little blue house. She let out a series of yips and waited for Leslie to appear.

Instead, a huge furry figure came barreling out of the front door, through a swinging black flap that Bella had not noticed before.

She couldn't believe her eyes.

"Leo?" she croaked.

As he bounded closer, Bella knew she was right. "Leo!" she cried again.

She was saved!

"Bella!" Leo barked, his wagging tail a blur. "Merry Christmas!"

She cringed. *Christmas? What does Leo know about Christmas?*

Nevertheless, she hobbled up to the picket fence

and allowed Leo to lick her face. His warm tongue felt ever so nice on her cold nose.

Then she collapsed on the ground. This way, the raw pads on the bottoms of her paws could finally get a break from the snow.

"What are you doing here?" she panted. "I thought you were with your pack!"

"No," Leo said. "I got nabbed by a dogcatcher. He took me back to the pound. But before I could run away again, Leslie adopted me."

Bella considered this.

"I thought you didn't *do* humans," she said.

"I don't," replied Leo. "But Leslie is different. She likes me just the way I am. She takes care of me. And lets me stay outside as much as I want. She even put in a door so I can go in and out whenever I like."

Leo's scar had healed, and his stomach had rounded out once again. This made Bella feel very happy for him. But it also made her feel even hungrier and lonelier than she had before. *Everyone has a family now but me,* she thought, ears drooping.

"Wait a minute!" Leo barked, cocking his head.

"What are *you* doing here?"

"I came to find Leslie," Bella replied. "I thought maybe she would give me something to eat. Then I was going to escape through the loose boards in the back."

"She replaced those when I came," Leo said. "But wait—why do you need Leslie to feed you? What about your humans?"

"They—they—they don't *want* me anymore!" howled Bella.

The awful truth sank its sharp teeth into her, biting deeper than the cold. She was never going back. Never going to see Alice and Andy again.

She was really and truly alone.

Leo bared his teeth. "Humans!" he snarled. "They're even worse than squirrels. Except for Leslie, of course. Is it because of the new baby?"

"Y-y-yes," whimpered Bella.

But then she had a thought.

"How do you know about the baby?"

"Leslie left yesterday morning," Leo said. "To go to the hospital. Your hu—er, Andy—called to tell her that he and Alice were there."

Bella jumped up, her heart suddenly racing. "Alice is in the hospital? Is she all right? Is the baby here?"

Leo shrugged his shoulders. "Leslie only came home late last night to sleep. By the time I woke up this morning, she was gone again. But you really shouldn't bother caring about those humans. They disgust me."

Bella heard a low growl in Leo's throat.

He was right. She should not care about Alice and Andy anymore. They had planned to take her to the pound. They had called her "Bad Bella." They had gone to the hospital to have their baby just as soon as she left. They had made it clear that she was once again unwanted.

So why do *I still care so much?*

Bella knew the answer, of course. She cared because she loved them. Would always love them. But they weren't hers any longer, and she had to think of the future now.

"Leo," Bella said, "can you tell me where I can find your pack?"

Leo opened his mouth and closed it again. Opened and closed it. Like he was trying to catch a fly.

"What's wrong?" Bella asked.

"I can tell you how to find them," Leo said finally. "But I don't know if that's such a good idea."

"They won't take me?" cried Bella. "They're my only hope! You were right all along about humans, Leo. And if I don't find your pack, I'll be caught and sent back to the pound. And then someone else will take me home and it will start all over. I can't do it again! I just can't!"

Leo sighed his mightiest sigh. "I'm sure they'll take you," he said. "But living on the streets is a hard life."

"You said you loved living with your pack!"

Leo hesitated. He looked down at his paws.

"That was before I found my home with Leslie."

Bella flopped back into the snow. "I know it won't be easy. But just tell me where they are."

Anything is better than being alone.

Leo nodded his head sadly. "I'll tell you. But first, let me go inside and get my food bowl. I'll bring it out so you can eat."

Bella waited on the other side of the fence while Leo shoved himself back through the doggy door and into the house to retrieve his bowl. She tried not to imagine how toasty warm it might be inside.

After he had returned and Bella had gulped down his breakfast, he tried once more to get her to change her mind.

"The pound won't be so bad," he said. "Maybe Leslie will take you in herself, and you can live with me!"

But Bella shook her head. Her mind was made up. So Leo began telling her everything she needed to know to find his pack. *Her* pack.

"I should go, Leo," she said when he was done. "Before someone sees me. Thanks for your help."

"You know where to find me now," he said. He kissed her nose goodbye.

"Tell Weasel I sent you," he called after her as she turned away. "And don't trust anything you hear from One-Eyed Nel. And never go near the man with the red apron, even though he smells like—"

Bella was too tired even to hear the rest of his warnings. She limped back through Leslie's quiet neighborhood, crouching low so as not to be seen by a family having a snowball fight in their yard.

If Andy and Alice had not decided to have a baby,

perhaps Bella and Andy would be playing the same game now, back in their park.

The thought was too much to bear. Andy and Alice had a new family, Bella reminded herself, and deep in the heart of the city there was a family of dogs waiting for her, too.

I just have to make it to them. . . .

Seventeen

The Long Road Home

Leo had told Bella that the dog pack sometimes spent winter nights in an alley between four restaurants. The heat from the kitchens spilled out into the alley, and there were always leftovers to be claimed in the trash heaps. Sometimes the scraps were even still warm.

To get to the alley, Bella would have to pass through her old neighborhood, close to Andy and Alice's apartment building, which meant she needed to be very, very careful not to be spotted by anyone who knew her. Then she would continue down past the park onto the busy street, which went all the way to a part of the city she did not know, but which she had seen in the distance because the buildings there were so tall.

Bella moved slower than ever now. The cold that had stung at her paws all day made its way into her knees and elbows, then to her hips and shoulders.

Each time she stopped, she had to rest for longer, and each time she rested, it became harder to pull herself up again. By the time it grew dark, she had only covered half the distance to her old home.

Bella looked behind her often to make sure no one was following. No one ever was.

This should have come as a relief, but it somehow made her feel worse.

Although she had seen very few cars and even fewer people outside, she began to notice all sorts of humans *inside*. Some houses had rows of candles dancing in the center window, while others had strings of light framing the door. Color spilled out onto the street from every house like bowls of melted candies.

In one house, humans sat around their dinner table, passing each other dishes of turkey and hot gravy that smelled delicious, even through the windows. In the next, the humans were curled up on the sofa together, watching a movie on TV. Through one window, Bella saw a family gathered around a glowing fireplace, each holding a stick with something fluffy and white on the end. Sounds of laughter and singing seemed to trickle out from each house she passed.

Bella thought of Andy and Alice. *Are they still at the hospital? Or are they home now? Are they gathered around the tree with their new baby? Have they even thought about me since I left?*

Most of all, she wondered about Alice. What if something had happened to her in the hospital? Or even to the baby? A knot of worry tightened in her stomach each time she thought about the possibiilty.

In fact, Bella was so worried that she had hardly noticed that, instead of sticking to Leo's directions, she had begun to follow her paws along the familiar roads that she and Andy used to run together. The next thing she knew, she was standing almost in front of their apartment building. She ducked quickly into the shadows on the other side of the street.

She couldn't believe herself. She was lucky no one had recognized her.

But now she was here, she thought, it couldn't hurt to stop a minute and take one last look at her old life.

Just to make sure Alice is all right.

Bella counted five windows up.

All she saw was a dark square.

No one was home.

Bella was so busy staring at the black window that she didn't notice the silver car pulling up across the street.

Eighteen

The Rose Family

The car door slammed, and Bella jumped.

Fortunately, she landed silently on her paws, which were quite numb by now.

When she got a better look at the car, she almost jumped again. *It's the Roses' car!*

Slowly, Bella retreated farther into the shadows.

Andy had gotten out of the car and was going around to the other side to help Alice.

The light inside the car was on, so Bella could see Alice's face. It was pale and tired.

When Andy held his hand out to her, she took it and stood.

Bella inched forward to get a closer look at Alice.

Just then, Alice glanced in her direction and frowned. Bella froze.

"What's wrong?" Andy asked.

"Nothing," Alice said, staring another moment before turning away. "I just thought I saw— Has there been any word from Leslie?"

Hearing Alice's voice made Bella's heart thump and ache at the same time. She knew she should slink away now. It wasn't safe to stay here. But her paws didn't seem to want to move.

"She's been putting posters up since yesterday morning," said Andy, who was fiddling now with a large gray basket on the seat. "But no one's called since the woman who saw Bella by the park yesterday afternoon."

"What if we don't find her? What if she doesn't come home?" asked Alice.

"We *will* find her," Andy said firmly. "I promise."

Home? What did Alice mean, home? Bella did not have a home anymore.

Do I?

Andy pulled the gray basket out from the car. Peeking out from the basket was a tiny blue bundle.

Bella couldn't take her eyes off it.

Suddenly the bundle began to cry.

Alice extended a finger toward it. "There, there," she cooed. "I know you want your big sister, Bella. It doesn't feel like Christmas without her, does it?"

Bella's ears perked up, and her heart began to race.

Sister?

She'd always thought the Roses treated her like their baby only because they didn't have one of their own. But if she was the baby's sister, then that meant that she really was . . . *family.*

Andy leaned over to kiss Alice on the cheek, and when he did, Bella saw a melted snowflake rolling down his face. She looked at Alice and saw that her face, too, was wet.

Not because of snowflakes, thought Bella suddenly. *Because of tears!*

They were crying because she was their baby, after all, and they missed her.

Bella took a small step forward. Then another. Until she was standing in the golden glow of the streetlight. But the Roses were looking the other way now. They were walking to the door of the apartment building. Another moment and they would disappear through it.

A small yip escaped from Bella's mouth.

Andy and Alice turned, and their eyes fell on her.

"Bella?" Alice whispered. "Is that you?"

Even though her paws were stiff, Bella broke into a run. She ran as fast as she could, and this time she knew where she was running.

Home.

In the blink of an eye, she had crossed the street and was standing in front of the Roses.

"*Bella!*" they shouted.

Their voices were filled with joy.

Andy knelt down and touched his face to Bella's.

"You scared us so much!" he said. But he didn't sound like he was scolding her at all.

Bella kissed him all over his cheeks and nose and chin to tell him that she was very sorry for running away.

I only did it because I was scared, too, she tried to say. *Because I thought you didn't want me anymore.*

Alice could not lean down, but when Bella looked up she saw that Alice was laughing and smiling her mightiest smile. "We love you so much, Bella," she murmured. Each quiet word hung in the air like a beautiful snowflake floating down from the sky. Bella wanted to catch each one and keep them in a place where they would never melt. "I don't know what we would do if we ever lost you again."

Bella sidled up to Alice to keep her warm and steady on her feet. She gently licked her palm. *You won't,* she said with her eyes, and she knew that Alice would understand. *I will never, ever leave you again.*

"It's a Christmas miracle!" Andy said, laughing. "But it's time to go inside now. Then once we're all warm, you can meet your new brother, Ben."

From the moment she walked in, Bella could tell that something was different in the apartment. Shiny packages had been placed under the Christmas tree. One of them was shaped and smelled suspiciously like a bone filled with peanut butter. Four colorful socks with fluffy white edges were hanging above the fireplace.

"I wanted everything to be just right for you when you got home," Alice said.

Andy laid the baby's basket down on the couch so that Bella could sniff Ben's fuzzy little head and stare at his scrunchy pink face.

He stared back at her with Andy's eyes and Alice's nose. He was a beautiful baby. And he smelled like both of them. Like home.

Bella loved him already.

Andy fixed Bella a bowl of warm milk and a heaping bowl of food. Then he dried her wet fur with a fluffy towel while she ate and drank.

"Poor girl," he said. "Your paws are freezing."

"Do you think we still need to take her to the vet?" Alice asked.

Bella's ears shot up. *The vet? Alice and Andy were planning to take me to* the vet?

Suddenly Bella remembered what Alice had said to Leslie the night Bella ran away. *We're going to have to take her in. . . . I know it's her least favorite place in the world, but it's best for her in the long run.*

Alice hadn't known that she was wrong. The vet

was *not* Bella's least favorite place in the world.

But Bella had been wrong, too. Alice had never considered taking Bella to the pound. All along, they were only going to take her to the vet!

"Let's see how she seems tomorrow," Andy said.

Bella wagged her tail. She was not worried. By tomorrow, Andy and Alice would see that there was no reason to take her to the vet. No reason to go anywhere at all, except perhaps the park to play snowballs.

After giving Bella two scoops of ice cream, Andy called Leslie to tell her that Bella had come home. "Yes, she's fine," he said. "Better than fine. She's perfect. Just like always."

Perfect, Bella repeated to herself. The strange word felt light and bubbly on her long tongue.

When Andy was done, he lifted Bella up and carried her to the bedroom. For a second, Bella's heart fell. Her round checkered bed had been moved away to make room for the baby's crib.

But then Andy laid her down at the foot of the bed.

Alice was resting with her head propped up on a stack of pillows, and she reached out her hand to rub behind Bella's ears.

"Ben has to sleep in here at first," she said. "So you'll just have to share with us."

Bella did not protest. The soft, warm bed was already soothing the aching cold from her body. Alice's foot made a very nice pillow indeed.

Andy brought Ben in, and Alice leaned over to kiss him on the head before Andy settled the baby into his crib.

When Andy climbed under the covers, he sighed a satisfied sigh. Then Alice sighed a happy sigh. Last, Bella sighed a grateful sigh. The baby was too young to sigh, but Bella knew he would if he were able.

"Just think, Bella," said Andy as he turned off the light. "A year ago you were being dropped off at the pound. And now here you are with us, and with a new baby brother."

"Right where you belong," Alice added.

Bella considered this. Deep into the night.

For so long, she had tried her very best to be a good dog. Ever since the McBrides had called her "Bad Bella" for the first time, she had been so afraid of disappointing her humans.

But Andy says I've always been perfect, Bella

thought. *So maybe I never really was a bad dog. Just like Hazel and Runt and Leo and Zoey weren't.*

Maybe just because someone tells you you're bad doesn't mean that you really are.

But, she thought too, she didn't always have to be on her best behavior, either. That's what it meant to belong somewhere. To be a part of a family.

It meant that Andy and Alice loved her for exactly who she was, the same way that Bella loved them.

It meant that being Bella was enough. Just Bella.

That night was the very last time Bella thought of the McBrides.

When she awoke the next morning, she would find she had much more important things to think about. Like being a big sister. Like showing Ben off to Leslie and Leo and Zoey. Like teaching her little brother how to fetch, and play snowballs, and run faster than the wind.

But all that would come later. For now, Bella snuggled deeper into the covers, listening to the gentle sounds of her sleeping family. Feeling full and happy and warm.

And wanted.

THE END

Author's Note

Dear Reader,

Hello! It's me, Ali Standish, the author of this book. Right now, I'm sitting in my office with the real-life Bella. She would say hello, too, but she is curled up in a neat little ball, fast asleep. She is also snoring, but please don't tell her I told you so, because she doesn't know she snores and would be very embarrassed to know the awful truth.

Yes, that's right, there is a real Bella, whose story inspired the one you just read. Perhaps you have paid too much attention in science class and are a bit confused about how the story of a dog who acts so much like a human could be true. Well, let me tell you.

When Bella and I first met, I had just graduated from college. I really, really loved college, by the way. (Unlimited ice cream! No parents to make you clean your room!

Classes that don't start until ten o'clock!) But one thing that I didn't like was that students were not allowed to have pets on campus. When I was growing up, my family had lots of pets, and I have always known that there is nothing quite like the love of a dog. So as soon as I graduated, found a place to live, and started my job as a teacher, I decided to look for a pup of my own.

My now husband, Aki, and I were living in Washington, DC. One crisp autumn Saturday, we drove out of the city and went to a few adoption fairs. At each one, there were so many wonderful dogs. But none that felt like *our* dog. Then, at the last fair, I was petting a very sweet black Labrador when Aki called me over.

"Ali," he said, "come meet this one!"

He was standing with a white dog that had black and brown spots and patches over her face and body—like an Oreo milkshake!—a big smile, and a fluffy tail that wagged so hard, her whole body shook. "What's her name?" I asked.

Well, you already know the answer to that.

Aki and I realized immediately that Bella was special. What other dog smiled like she did? What other dog wagged so hard? Bella didn't need to wrap her leash in circles around us (she did anyway). By then, we already knew we were going to take her home.

Bella had been living with a wonderful foster mom, and when we told her that we wanted to adopt Bella, tears welled in her eyes. "She's the best dog I've ever fostered," she said. "I don't know why it's taken so long for someone to adopt her."

We didn't, either. But we are grateful every day.

On the car ride home, Bella sat in the back, first with her head out the window and her wet nose twitching, then curled up on the seat.

It was after she had fallen asleep that I took out the little folder of information that the rescue organization had given us. Inside was a glimpse at Bella's past, including a form that had been filled out by the man who had dropped Bella off at the pound.

When I saw the date she had been left there, my heart suddenly felt all strange and splintery, like it was going to crack. December twenty-second. Three days before Christmas.

The man wrote two other things that stuck out to

me. One was that he was Bella's owner. The other was that she was not his dog.

I didn't understand how both of those things could be true. How could you own a dog and say she wasn't yours?

Unlike Bella in the story, our Bella was removed from the pound by an animal rescue organization, the Lost Dog & Cat Rescue Foundation of Virginia. They took care of her and eventually placed her with her foster mom, which is where she lived until we found her, ten months after she had been abandoned.

It didn't take long after adopting Bella for Aki and me to realize that welcoming her into our family was the best decision we had ever made. We loved her unconditionally, right from the start. But it's hard to get a dog to understand that kind of love when she's been abandoned before. It was obvious that Bella loved her new home—loved our walks, loved the park, loved the belly and behind-the-ear scratches she got several times a day.

But she was also still very shy. She would not get up on the furniture, even when she was invited. She was afraid of loud noises. And once, when we came home, it was to find that she had had a big, messy, smelly accident on the apartment floor. (I think you know what kind I mean. . . .) She greeted us with her tail between her legs, and she had even tried to cover her accident up with a shoe! Could I have imagined the relief in her eyes when we told her we weren't mad at her, when we petted her gently instead of yelling at her? Maybe. But I don't think so.

Soon it was Christmastime. Our first Christmas as a family. I have always loved Christmas. (The cookies! The presents! The snow!) Most of all, I love Christmas trees. I love everything about them! Picking them out, decorating them, putting presents underneath them. I love their sharp, sweet smell.

Bella did *not* like our tree.

In fact, she would not even go near it. Instead, she stared at it from across the apartment with narrowed eyes. Like it might attack her at any moment.

"Why do you think she acts that way around the tree?" Aki asked.

I wasn't sure, but I had a guess.

"Maybe her old family had a Christmas tree," I said. "They would have put it up right around the time they dropped her off at the pound. Maybe seeing another one makes her nervous because she thinks it means we're about to do the same thing."

We weren't, of course. But that's when I started to think of this story.

There are lots of reasons that someone might not be able to care for their dog any longer, and I can't know or judge Bella's original owner's reasons for leaving her at the pound. But I *do* know that lots of people adopt dogs with good intentions, only to realize that owning a dog is too much of a responsibility. So I imagined a family—the McBrides—who had grown too busy to take care of their dog. I imagined how confused Bella must have been to find herself at the pound, and how she must have searched for a reason why she had been abandoned. How she couldn't have known that it wasn't her fault, that *it is never your fault when someone bigger than you leaves you behind or stops loving you.*

Little by little, our Bella began to realize that we would never stop loving her. She didn't mind when we left her in the apartment while we went to work, because she knew we would come home again. She also knew that when her paws grew too cold in the snow, Aki would carry her home. She even started sleeping on the bed. Right in the middle. Taking up half the mattress. Snoring. Loudly.

By the next Christmas, Bella wasn't quite so nervous around the tree, maybe because her memory of whatever came before we adopted her was starting to fade away. And now Christmas is one of Bella's favorite times of the year. (The cookies! The presents! The snow!)

In her time with us, Bella has been on many adventures. She has been to baseball games, climbed mountains, and gone kayaking. She has lived on two different continents and sailed across the Atlantic on a cruise ship. No matter where Bella goes, people always comment on what a friendly, smiley dog she is. She doesn't have any human siblings, but last year she got a doggy brother, Keeper. He loves his big sister more than anyone else in the world.

Throughout our years together, I have marveled many times at the way Bella so often seems to know exactly what I'm thinking. And the way I understand her almost as if she were speaking to me in plain English. Aki says she is my doggy soul mate. Neither of us wants to imagine what our lives would have been like if he hadn't spotted Bella that day.

And after all this time, I understand why her first owner wrote that she was not his dog.

Because she wasn't. All along, even before we ever met her, she had been ours. All that time, we had been hers, too.

And we always will be.

Bella enjoys a car ride just a few days after we adopted her.

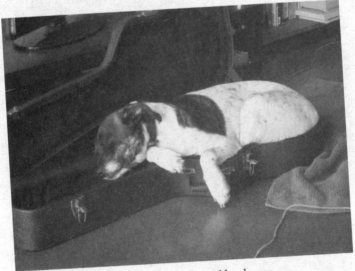

It wasn't long before she made herself at home.

Bella and Aki love playing fetch together.

Everywhere we go, people comment on Bella's smile!

And she always enjoys a good snow day.

Bella has seen the ocean . . .

. . . and the mountains, too!

We even sailed from the UK to the US on the *Queen Mary II.*

(All those adventures can make you pretty tired.)

Bella's latest adventure has been becoming a sister to Keeper. He thinks she's the best big sister ever.

One Last Thing . . .

Our Bella found her forever home, but there are millions of dogs (and cats! bunnies! pigs! and others!) who are still waiting in shelters around the country to find their humans. Here are some things you can do to make a difference in their lives:

- Donate your birthday. Instead of receiving gifts yourself, ask a local animal shelter what supplies they need, and ask friends and family to buy those. Some shelters may even let you host your party there—or bring animals out to your party to say thanks! And what better party favor could you give than a puppy or kitten cuddle?!
- Collect old linens. Animal shelters are often in need of things like blankets, sheets, and towels to keep their animals warm and comfortable.

Organize a donation drive where people can bring their old linens to you to take to a shelter instead of just throwing them out.

* Host a bake sale! But instead of cookies and cakes, bake doggy biscuits for all the dog lovers out there who are likely to want to support your cause. Donate the profits to your local shelter or humane society.

* Follow your local shelter or humane society on social media, and share the work they are doing with your own network. The more awareness they get, the more animals they can save!

* Talk with your family about fostering an animal. Lots of animals, like Bella, have foster parents who take care of them while they wait to be adopted. This creates more room in the shelters for other animals who need a safe place. Fostering can be a great way to help an animal in need of some love without the long-term commitment of adopting.

* But if you and your family are (really, really) ready to give an animal a forever home, adopt from a shelter or humane society instead of buying from a pet shop or breeder. Animals in pet shops often

come from puppy mills or kitten factories, places that don't treat animals very kindly. (Happily, there are some exceptions to this, as in California, where pet stores can sell only rescue animals!) Instead of spending money to support those businesses, head to your local shelter and support all the work they do to help animals. When you take an animal home from a shelter, you make space for another dog to be rescued.

🐾 Get in touch with your lawmakers. States, and even cities, have different laws about things like puppy mills. Write or call your local and state lawmakers and ask that they pass a law that requires pet stores to sell rescued animals instead of ones that come from puppy mills or kitten factories. If these mills and factories don't have anyone left to sell their animals to, they will have to shut down for good. Then there will be fewer animals to rescue in the long run, and more animals who can enjoy forever homes!

Acknowledgments

As ever, I am hugely grateful for my agents, Sarah Davies and Polly Nolan, for championing my writing and this manuscript. To Alyson Day, for loving Bella's story, and giving me the opportunity to share it with the world. To the whole team at Harper, for working so hard to make this novel the best it could be: Manny Blasco, Megan Ilnitzki, Renée Cafiero, Laura Mock, Amy Ryan, and Vaishali Nayak. And to Melissa Manwill for giving this book a beautiful cover, and for capturing the real Bella's spirit while also rendering her into a new, highly lovable character.

I started writing this book in the summer of 2014 in Claudia Mills's chapter books class at Hollins University, and I owe her a special thanks for crying over the very first draft of the very first chapter and telling me to keep writing. I'm thankful, too, for all the feedback

I received on early drafts from my fellow students Amy Deligdisch, Amy DeBevoise, Lucy Hester, Jennifer Sigler, Audrey Hackett, and Caity Neilands. And to Nancy Ruth Patterson, for jumping on the Bella bandwagon so enthusiastically and embracing the story as only a true dog lover could.

This book could never have happened without the real Bella, and so I want to thank all those who helped her come into our lives and who have loved and cared for her alongside us over the years. There are too many to name individually, but I do want to mention the Lost Dog & Cat Rescue Foundation for rescuing Bella from the pound and giving her a second chance at life; Melissa Poulin for providing her with a loving foster home; Harri Laakso for forgiving us for not taking his dog advice; Julie Mitchell and her Zoey for being Bella's best ever playdates; Ritva Laakso, Jacobo Caballeiro, and Leidy Suarez for caring for her so tenderly and helping her to heal from her hip surgery; Kevin Cusick for making sure she would always be able to run; John Lester and Kevin Bull for giving her a second home and family in Grantchester; and Mom and Dad for helping every step along the way.

And, of course, to Aki Laakso, who knew right away that Bella belonged with us, who has been the most loving and devoted doggy daddy a pup could ask for, and who has loved this book since the very first word. Thank you for choosing our girl.